To O...

my good friend

Margaret Bowling

# Mountain Refuge

by

## Margaret Bowling

ISBN 978-0-7414-7765-1

Printed in the United States of America

Published August 2012

INFINITY PUBLISHING
1094 New DeHaven Street, Suite 100
West Conshohocken, PA 19428-2713
Toll-free (877) BUY BOOK
Local Phone (610) 941-9999
Fax (610) 941-9959
Info@buybooksontheweb.com
www.buybooksontheweb.com

*To Joe---who gave encouragement and hope*

# Chapter
# ONE

Will took the two water pails to the spring. He wanted to take the walk one more time and look around, as he was leaving the mountain, and didn't know when he would be back again. His bags were packed and waiting. He spotted a deer in the bushes, "Don't worry little fellow," he said. "You need not fear me. I leave the mountains to you."

.   He had been born here in these mountains of Scott County, Tennessee. He had studied hard and it was time to go.

He picked up the pails and filled them with cold spring water and returned to the cabin. His mother was weeping, and his father and brothers, Jesse and Hugh, were sitting and staring into the fire. Will set the pails on the work table. He said to Jane, his mother, "Now, Ma, don't cry. You know I have to leave."

"I know, Will, but it is so hard to see you go. I know you want to study in Alabama. You will write every chance you get, won't you?"

"Of course, and I'll be back to see you some time." We better go, Son," said William Wilson, Senior, his father. "The stagecoach won't wait."

Will dozed off and on during the night as the stagecoach traveled through woods and valleys. He looked out when they passed inns that showed lanterns in windows and sometimes stopped to take on passengers. The seat was uncomfortable. He shifted to get in a better position, and then dozed again. The coach pulled into a Stagecoach Inn, and the driver told the passengers to alight and go in for a meal. Will was sore from the bumpy ride, but he managed to get inside, and have a big meal of beef and potatoes and dark coffee. He walked outside for a few minutes. The fresh horses were hitched up and the coach loaded once more. The new passengers were one elderly gentleman, and two young ladies dressed in dark serge with straw bonnets and valises. After a few minutes of chatting, the darkness of the road caused them to doze once more. When Will awoke the next time, they were outside the Morly Stage Inn and Tavern. The drivers got down from their perch, and Will was handed his bag from the rack above. "We will finish the night here," said the man. "We leave at dawn. Tell the innkeeper to wake you in time to eat and freshen up."

Will went inside and learned the dining room was closed. He rented a room for the night and was shown upstairs. He propped a chair under the door knob to discourage thieves and climbed into the bed.

A loud knock disturbed his sleep and immediately he was up. "Time to get up, Mr. Wilson." Will threw water from the pitcher on to his face and decided not to take time to shave. He needed coffee more. So taking his case, he descended the stairs and found the dining room open. The two drivers were there having breakfast of ham and eggs, biscuits and jelly, and strong coffee.

Will sat down and immediately was served the same. The driver next to his chair said "We leave in twenty minutes. Eat up, and pay up front."

Outside, the man and two ladies were waiting to board. The man told him, "We didn't take down our luggage because we get off at the next stop.

One of the ladies asked, "Did you sleep well?"

"Yes, but not enough," he laughed and so did she.

"We depart the stage at Cooper's landing."

"I go on to Birmingham," said Will.

"We took on fresh horses here," said one of the drivers. "We should make good time, Mr. Weaver."

They climbed on board the stage and settled for the trip. "May I introduce my nieces? Misses Mary and Jewel Landstrom."

Will extended his hand. "William Wilson, Sir. Glad to meet you and the young ladies."

The morning was glorious, and Will felt more rested now. The coffee had boosted his strength. He watched the scenery from the window with interest. It was flatter here, and looked very lush and green. The air was fresh too. He breathed it in deeply.

"We live just ten miles from here," said Miss Jewel.

"I hope you have had a safe journey."

"We have indeed," said the girl. "Our uncle has been very kind to have us travel with him. We live fairly near the Inn. If you'd care to visit some time."

"If I am ever up this way, I'd be delighted to do that."


Will arrived in Birmingham. It was a beautiful day. He saw a diner just down the street. He picked up his bag, and started walking. It was pleasant inside, and he ordered coffee and a breakfast of bacon and eggs. The waitress smiled and noticed his bag near the door. "Welcome to Birmingham," she said.

"Thanks," he answered, and started to drink the hot coffee while he waited for his breakfast.

"How long before the town starts stirring?" he asked.

"About dawn," she answered. "Maybe an hour."

"Can you direct me to a boarding house or a hotel?" he asked her.

"Sure. Just about two blocks down there is a hotel, and there is a boarding house on the next street over on the East side. It is 1100 Main Street."

"Thanks," he said.

When she brought his breakfast, he said, "This looks good."

After having his second cup of coffee Will could see pale streaks of light and knew it would soon be dawn. He paid his tab and started for the door.

Outside, he carried his bags for two blocks and saw the street sign. "Main Street." He saw 1100 right away, and went up the wide steps. A sign said "Enter". Will went in to the long hallway, and a bell jingled over the door. A man appeared.

Will asked for the rates of the rooms, and finding them reasonable, he rented one on the second floor for one week. Soon he was upstairs and sound asleep in the big four poster bed.

The street noises awoke Will. He went to eat in the dining room, where he met other boarders and asked some questions about the town. He needed a good map and was told where to get one. He met Mrs. Shelton, a short happy faced woman, who served the meal.

Will took a walk around the neighborhood to get familiar with the streets. He bought a map at the post office, and bought some postcards to send home. He returned to the boarding house to learn where the bathing facilities were. He took a bath and went to his room to write postcards home.

At breakfast the next morning, he asked the other boarders if there were carriages and drivers for hire and where to find them.

Soon he was on his way to the address he sought. The offices were located in a two storied brick building, and he alighted from the carriage and climbed the steps. He found the name that was familiar on the registry, and entered the office. He was shown in to meet Mr. Timothy Field who was a distinguished, tall gentleman with a white beard.

"Mr. Wilson, I have been expecting you," Mr. Field said. "I have letters from an old friend in Scott County, Tennessee, and he speaks very well of you. Have a seat."

Will handed Mr. Field the letters of recommendation, and waited.

"Tell me a little about yourself, Mr. Wilson." Whereupon Will told him of his great uncles in North Carolina, who had been judges and lawyers, and of his ambitions to study law.

"Mr. Porter said you have done some studying since you left school, and borrowed some of his law books."

"Yes, Sir, and I studied with a former teacher to prepare myself. She taught me to improve my handwriting and public speaking, since I would need those talents."

"I have read all this material about you, and I want to hear your reasons for wanting to start here to learn the business."

Will discussed all that had led him to Alabama. "I would like to work with you and learn all I can, and eventually pass the bar. I want to practice law in Alabama."

"I will discuss this with my associates and meet with you tomorrow at eight, if that is satisfactory with you." He stood and shook hands with Will. "Then I will see you tomorrow."

Will was very excited. "One more day," he thought, "and I will know for sure." He went out and hired a carriage and drove around just to see the countryside. "Out here somewhere I will build my new home. I will be a success." Will turned back to town. "I must get some letters off," he said to himself.

During the next weeks, Will went with Mr. Field to trials and hearings, sat in on discussions and later discussed them with his mentor. Mr. Field set up an account for Will at the bank in town, and ordered a carriage for his use. Will was so happy he wrote home to tell his parents that he was on his way to being a lawyer.

Will left the boarding house and took rooms near the Courthouse. He ate at hotels and diners and met as many people as he could.

Months later he was on an assignment to Elyton, Alabama, a small town in beautiful farming country. He consulted his map and made his way to the correct address. He was making excellent time.

Upon finishing his assignment, he left the building, and walked to his carriage. He noticed a young lady coming down the street carrying several packages, and looked in danger of losing half of them. "What a beautiful young lady," thought Will. As the girl approached one of her parcels dropped to the ground, and Will at once went to help her.

"Please, allow me," he said, and picked up the package from the street.

At first the woman was startled, but Will smiled his brightest. "Don't be alarmed," he said. "My name is William Wilson, and I am employed by Field and Associates. I can assure you I am quite reliable."

"I am Lydia George. My brother is waiting for me at the hotel, and I am late. Thanks very much."

At the hotel, Will opened the door for her and followed, carrying some of her packages for her. She saw her brother at a table near the window.

"There is Thomas now," she said. She hurried over, where the young man stood at once. Lydia introduced her brother and said, "Thomas, this is William Wilson. He has been nice enough to help me with my packages when they started to fall."

Thomas said, "Won't you join us for coffee?"

"Of course. Thank you." He helped Lydia to her chair, and sat across from her.

Will explained his position in Birmingham, and told them he was from upper Tennessee.

Thomas informed Will that he and Lydia lived with their parents who owned a plantation a few miles east of the town. They were Anna and Lewis George. After Lydia and Will had finished their coffee, Thomas said they should be going. Will said, "I would consider it an honor if I could see you again, Miss George."

"Call me Lydia, please."

"Thank you again for helping my sister," said Thomas. "Perhaps you would like to stop by our home on East Elyton Road some time?"

"Would this Sunday be too soon?" asked Will with a chuckle. Thomas gave him directions and they rose to leave. Will shook hands again with Thomas and bowed to Lydia. They walked outside together. Thomas admired Will's black carriage. They parted and Will was elated to get back to Birmingham, and think about this day and to marvel at the opportunity he had experienced to meet this beautiful girl with the sparkling blue eyes and hair as brown as a sparrow's wing.

The following Sunday, Will drove out to Elyton. It was a clear morning, the breeze causing the leaves to tremble on the trees. Will was a little nervous. He was a man from the mountains. He hoped he could remember his manners at the home of Lydia George.

He followed directions and turned in at the gate. The drive was tree-lined and spread with gravel. He followed it up to the front of the two story white house, and tied his horses to a hitching rail. The veranda was wide, with wicker furniture, and blooming plants hanging from hooks. Will climbed the steps and approached a massive door with a knocker shaped like an eagle.

Will paused, then took a deep breath and lifted the knocker. A tall woman in a gray dress covered with a starched white apron opened the door. "I am Mr. Wilson, calling on Miss Lydia George."

The woman stepped back and Will entered. She softly closed the door and took his hat, then placed it on the hall table.

"Please come this way."

"They entered the large room where the George family was seated, and the woman, said. "Mr. Wilson."

Thomas arose at once and shook hands with Will. "Father, this is William Wilson,"

Will stepped forward and shook hands with Lewis George. "Will, this is my father and mother, Lewis and Anna George. We are glad you could come."

Lydia said, "William, please come sit here by me. Father, this is the gentleman that I told you about. William, I am so glad to see you. Please meet my sister, Mary."

Will bowed to Mary and said, "I am so pleased to meet you."

"I understand from my son that you are from Tennessee?"

"Yes, sir. Upper East Tennessee, close to the Kentucky line. I came to Alabama to study law."

"You made a wise choice."

"Do you have family back in Tennessee?" asked Mrs. George.

"Yes. My parents and two brothers."

They talked for a long while, then a servant came in and announced dinner. Will escorted Lydia and followed Mr. and Mrs. George into the dining room. It was a spacious room well-lighted, and pleasant. Food was simple, hot and delicious. Will thoroughly enjoyed his visit and was invited back.

During the next few weeks Will was kept quite busy. He attended hearings, trials, and met with Mr. Field's witnesses prior to the trials. He met judges and other people connected to his business. Will learned quickly, and Mr. Field was very pleased with him.

Will spent many Sunday afternoons at the George home. He took Lydia out to dine at the hotels and various restaurants. Mr. George was very pleased that Will seemed to be admired by his daughter. He talked with Anne at length about it.

"I think Will may ask for Lydia's hand soon. Do you think I should agree?"

Anna answered, "I do like this young man. He's serious and already on his way to being an attorney. He would make Lydia a fine husband."

Lewis agreed, "He certainly has won over Lydia!"

*Chapter*

# TWO

One day Mr. Field called for his secretary. He was feeling weak. "I think we should have a doctor, Mrs. Keene."

At once Mrs. Keene rushed out and sent word by an assistant to go up the street for Dr. Turner. As Will returned from an errand, he was shocked to find the doctor's buggy in front of the building and to learn inside that Mr. Field had become ill. He waited anxiously outside the office door for the doctor.

Mr. Field was assisted out to his carriage, and Will approached Dr. Turner. "I am an assistant of Mr. Field, Sir. Can you tell me anything at all?"

"Mr. Field has some problems. He has been working too hard with little rest. I have recommended that he stay home for a few days, and I will tend him there. You may call on him tomorrow along with his secretary for instructions."

Will was scared. Mr. Field had been his employer, teacher, benefactor, and a dear friend. They closed the offices, after straightening up a few affairs.

Mr. Field had been home for several days, and his associates had managed all the cases, Dr. Turner allowed Mr.

Field to return to his offices. He stayed for only a few hours each day.

One day Mr. Field called Will in to speak with him. "Will, I would like to meet this girl of yours. You have done an excellent job of helping out Mr. Ellis and Harvey in my absence."

"Thank you, Sir. I would be happy for you to meet Lydia. I am going to ask her to marry me."

"Come in tomorrow and see me. We will arrange a day and time to have a meal."

Will went to see Lydia and asked if she could come to dinner in Birmingham that Friday. He explained that Mr. Field wanted to meet her. He also spoke to her father. "I will escort Lydia and be responsible for her."

On Friday, at the Sirgoine Hotel, Mr. Field and his two associates sat with Lydia and Will. She was introduced to the lawyers. They had dinner in the dining room. It was a pleasant evening, and Will arranged for Lydia to stay overnight at the hotel. He booked separate rooms so he could be close by. The next morning he took her to breakfast and informed his employer that he would like to take the time to drive her home.

He pulled over to a little park where they strolled for a time arm in arm. Then Will asked Lydia if she would marry him. "Lydia, you mean the world to me, and I want very much for you to be my wife. If Lewis agrees, may we go pick out a ring?"

Lydia said, "Yes, Will, I will marry you. I love you so much, and I really do want to be your wife." After an embrace they walked back to the carriage.

"I am anxious now to get to Lewis and get his permission," Will said. They found both Lewis and Anne on the front veranda, and climbed up the steps smiling.

"Mr. George, I have asked Lydia to be my wife. Will you give me her hand in marriage?"

"Has she said 'yes' to you?" asked Lewis, laughing heartily.

"Yes, Father," said Lydia, "I have said 'yes'." She went around and hugged her mother.

"Well, Son, I do give my blessing. You are a fine gentleman, and I think both of you will be very happy together."

Will said goodnight to them all, and asked Lydia to walk with him to the carriage.

"Would you want to go with me to choose a ring or would you want me to get it in Birmingham?"

"You go on, Will. I know I will be happy with what you choose."

"Now you must be thinking of a date for us," said Will. He kissed her goodbye, now not caring who saw them, for now they were betrothed.

Will and Lydia were married. The little church was decorated with flowers. Lydia wore a long white gown with a veil of lace. Mary George was her maid of honor and Timothy Field was Will's best man. Lydia carried a bouquet of pink rosebuds, and a white prayer book.

The wedding party went to the George home for a reception. There they were toasted by his law firm associates, and best wishes were given all around. Then Lydia changed into a dove gray dress with lace collar and they slipped away, leaving and the family and others still celebrating. Will took her to his rooms in Birmingham. He left her there to go and stable his horses.

When he returned he embraced and kissed Lydia. "Well, Mrs. Wilson, we did it. You have become my wife. You have made me the happiest man in the world."

Lydia answered, "And I am the happiest woman. And the luckiest, I might add, to be married to a most handsome man!"

"You flatter me, Mrs. Wilson, but I like it"

During the following days Lydia cooked for them on a little stove and kept the rooms clean. They were very happy, but Lydia missed her family terribly.

For several weeks, Mr. Field cut his working days shorter, and Will took on more and more work. The other partners did the bulk of the business, and Will learned more from them. Will sold his carriage and bought a little black buggy that Lydia could drive when she chose. He walked to the offices on pleasant days, and used the buggy when there was rain.

One day Mr. Field collapsed in the chair of his office. His secretary sent out the alarm to the other lawyers and everyone came running. Mr. Field grabbed the area around his heart. Will and the others lay him on the floor and sent for the doctor. Dr. Turner came at once but it was too late. Will was devastated. He rushed home to Lydia and grieved. He was numb and sat staring straight ahead. Lydia tried to comfort him. He was so grieved that he did nothing for hours. What would happen to them now?

The law offices were closed, and a black wreath placed on the door. Another was placed on the door of the Field home.

At the funeral Will could only stare ahead, his heart like a stone within him. Lydia sat beside him, dressed in black. She hurt for him, and tried to console him. Mr. Field had been so close to Will that he mourned him as much as if he had been his father.

After several days, Harold Stevens told Will he had the will, and they must meet in Mr. Field's office. Woodenly, he went along. He saw Mrs. Agatha Gray sitting on a leather chair weeping into her handkerchief. She was Mr. Field's housekeeper. He went to her and laid a hand on her shoulder. He couldn't speak. She reached up and patted his hand. Will took his seat and waited. Harold cleared his throat and began. "I, being of sound mind---"

Will's mind drifted off. It was not right that Harold was sitting in Mr. Field's chair behind his desk. Nothing seemed right. Then he heard Harold say, "To my housekeeper and friend, Agatha Louise Gray, I leave my house on Main Street, and a pension of $500 annually. The remainder of my estate I leave to William J. Wilson, Jr."

Will was stunned. he stared straight ahead. It couldn't be!Mr. Fields couldn't have done this. He didn't realize that his employer, his old friend would make such a gift to him. I must go tell Lydia!

In the autumn, Will passed the bar exam, and received his license to practice law in the state of Alabama. Lydia and Lewis and Anna George were there for the swearing in ceremony when Will took the required oath. "It is done," said Lewis. "You are an attorney. We must celebrate!" He hugged his son-in-law. "We will go have dinner and the bill is on me!"

# Chapter
# THREE

Lydia had brought her servant, Savannah, from her father's plantation. Savannah had been Lydia's nurse when she was a child, and Savannah was very fond of her. Lydia needed help now, as Will planned their future.

Will said, "We must move to a larger house. I will start searching for property soon."

For some time Lewis George had wanted Will to buy land close to his property. Now he suggested that Will buy a section of his own land. I will make you a good offer, and it will keep my family close to me. "We will all benefit from it," Lewis told him.

Will agreed. They drew up papers, and the deal was settled to everyone's satisfaction.

Lydia was so happy to know she would be near her mother and sister. Anna and Mary were delighted, too. They looked forward to many happy days.

Thomas had bought property also, near his father, and his house was nearly finished. He and his fiance were married in the same church where they had attended Will's and Lydia's wedding. Lydia was the matron of honor, and James was his brother's best man.

When Lydia was sick for three mornings in a row, she suspected the reason. She went to see Dr. Turner and was told that she indeed was with child. She and Savannah prepared a special dinner for Will that night, complete with lighted candles. Savanna ate early and retired to her room. As Will entered and removed his coat and hat, he asked," Are we having a party?"

"Yes, a party for two. After they had eaten, Lydia said, "It is actually a party for three. I saw Dr. Turner today, and he says we are expecting a baby."

Will was ecstatic and danced around the room and kissed Lydia. "I am a very happy man, Lydia. Just think a little boy!"

"Or a girl. Will, it may be a girl."

In Roane County, Tennessee, William Wilson, Senior stepped out on his porch. He saw the morning glories that Jane had transferred from the fence row to the front yard. They were blooming in various colors and were gorgeous. He was glad he had sold out in Scott County, and bought this property. It was fertile land and stretched out on flatter ground, and he gloried in the rows of vegetables and the fields beyond where the corn was high.

William spotted his son, Jesse, riding in from the road, and waited for him. He had a letter for his father in his hand. "It's from Will," he said.

William opened the envelope and read.

"Dear Mother and Papa, It is with great joy that I am writing today. Lydia has told me she is expecting a child. She is feeling fine, and wants you both to know how happy she is.

We are planning to build a house near the George family, and we plan to come and visit you and the family at the earliest possible time. We are hoping you are well. We are fortunate to have done well here, and we send our love to you both. Write us soon. Tell Hugh and Jesse that I long to see them again. Mother, I love you, and will come to you as soon as I can. Affectionately, Your son, Will."

15

Will's house went up quickly. He had a carriage house built behind it, with living quarters above for the driver of his carriages. He planned to hire workmen later to work on the land and to raise cattle.

Lydia visited with her mother and sister and sister-in-law. They sewed and embroidered lacy little gowns and clothes for the baby. Anna was very happy and so was Thomas' wife. They were merry and chatted and had a wonderful time together. "I hope your first is a boy, Lydia," said her mother.

Mary said, "And I am hoping it is a girl!"

Will's law practice grew, and he was getting a good reputation in the city. Many of Mr. Field's friends recommended customers to him, and he was popular. He and Lydia joined a church, and took Savannah with them to services. His farm prospered, and he looked forward to the birth of his child.

Sometimes his hours were long, and some days he sat wearily with his paper in the evenings. Occasionally, a trial would go badly. These would depress him, but he knew that all his cases would not be successful.

Will delighted in his family. He now had the daughter he had longed for, the pride and joy of Anne who made dresses and linen petticoats with embroidered hems and bodices for little Martha. Dent had grown brown and sturdy from his days outdoors and Will was very proud of them both.

Will met with his caretaker in the carriage house and always got good reports. New calves were dropped and the stock multiplied, and the fields were green with healthy crops of corn and potatoes. Soon he promised himself, he would take his family to meet the folks in Tennessee.

More and more cases came Will's way. He thought of adding a young apprentice as he had been when he came to Birmingham.

His son, George, was born one cool night and there was pandemonium in the house. Anna took the children to the plantation house to keep them away from all the distress. Lydia's mother had moved in, and she and Savannah needed all their strength to keep up with the demands. More help was brought in and the baby finally made his way into the world at last.

"We will name him George," said Lydia.

Will kissed her brow. "Anything you say, dear. You have been through so much."

"Papa will like that, don't you think?"

"He will, I am sure. We have two fine sons now."

The child grew strong, and was the delight of all the George clan. Anna and Thomas, with his wife came often and took the children on picnics and outings, sometimes kept them overnight. Lydia's mother had ladies in to tea and paraded her grandchildren around so proudly. "I am afraid I spoil them terribly," she said.

When little George wailed with teething pains she cut a beech twig and rubbed on his gums to quiet him. This allowed Lydia to sew her dainty undergarments and special linens as she directed her servants in the kitchen at her own time. The canning and preserving went on under Savannah's watchful eye.

# Chapter
# FOUR

The courtroom was hot and stuffy. For four days the trial had gone on. The jury members were tired and longed for relief from the heat.

Laman Deems was sitting belligerently at the table with his lawyer, confident that he would be found innocent. He had been in several barroom fights, and was a vicious hard-hearted man. His brothers and father had bragged that he would go free. Will Wilson was equally sure that he would be convicted of assault and spend time in jail. That afternoon a new witness had appeared. This tipped the scales in William's favor.

The verdict was "Guilty." Laman's family was furious! The judge ordered that they be removed from the courtroom to keep peace. Will was glad it was finally over, and went home to be with his family.

Lydia wiped the sweat from her brow, and bent over the wash tub. It was nearing noon and she still had clothes to hang on the line between the trees in the back. The clothes line was already full with her morning's work: the long dresses and shirts flying in the breeze and soaking up the sun. She loved the smell of sun dried clothes. Her two oldest, Dennis, who was known as Dent, and Martha were playing in the yard, and she knew they would be getting hungry soon. She wiped her hands on her apron and went inside. Her two youngest, George and John were napping. The stew was simmering there on the big iron cook stove. She pulled open the oven door and removed a skillet of cornbread she had made earlier for their dinner. Martha and Dent ran in and washed their hands at the wash stand. "Hurry now," said Lydia. "Get to the table. I still have a lot of wash to do. I can't be dilly-dallying around."

The stew tasted good with cornbread and cold milk. There was plenty for supper. She wouldn't have time to cook again after she gathered in the clothes and scrubbed her kitchen with the sudsy water still in the tub. Washday was hard but she liked to do her own work when she felt well enough to do it. Her old nurse, Savannah was retired with rheumatism which made it too hard for her to work any longer. "I will sure sleep well tonight," she thought. Since Savannah had left to go to live with her daughter, Lydia worked very hard to keep her family fed and clean.

Lydia was pulling down the last of the shirts from the rope clothes line when she saw Daisy Wells coming from the side of the house. "That's strange," thought Lydia. Daisy never comes by this time of day."

"Let me help you with these things," she said. "I need to talk to you."

After they were seated inside, Daisy said, "Lydia, that man Rafe Deems has been bragging he was going to get even with Will for the sentence his brother got in the courtroom. We must get over to the George house at once," she said. "Mr. George will send someone for Will." Daisy took Lydia and the children to the George home in her little buggy.

They sat and talked, and Anne served them lemonade. Lewis heard what they had to say. "It could be serious, Lydia You take the children home and wait. I'll go after Will, and we will talk."

Will sat with his father-in-law and discussed the situation. Will said, "Lewis, I just can't take this man seriously. He likes to brag and he is a very disagreeable person. However, I don't think his anger would go that far. Laman was found guilty of robbery and assault by a jury. I did not cause the sentence he got."

"I know that, Will. I am thinking of my daughter and my grandchildren."

"I will go talk to Rafe. I will convince him his brother is guilty as charged."

Lewis threw up his hands, "Will, you are talking about a whole family who think nothing of violent crime. There are dozens of the clan. Listen to me. They mean business!"

"All right, Lewis. I will go home and talk to Lydia. We will work something out and get back to you."

That night Lydia was worried as she lay beside Will and stared at the dark window, unable to sleep. Will had refused to believe that Rafe and his family would be that dangerous. She had put the baby John who was one year old to bed, and had to rock little George to sleep. He seemed to know that Lydia was worried. At last he was asleep and Lydia went to bed, but had a hard time falling asleep.

As she finally dozed off, there was a loud knock on the door. Will was the first to reach the front windows and look out at the moonlit porch where Lewis stood. Will threw open the door.

"Will, you have to hurry. There isn't a lot of time. I have my wagon outside. Get the children up quickly and get them dressed. Lydia, put some things in a pillow case and put some pillows and quilts in the wagon." Stunned, Lydia stared at her father.

"Hurry up, girl. Will, Rafe has gone to get his brothers who live five miles from here. One of the men came and told me because he didn't want to see you killed. Will threw on his clothes and grabbed his gun from the mantel piece.

"I don't want to run, Lewis," he said.

"You have to think of the children, Will. There isn't time to get ready for a fight. You must protect your family."

"Do you really think they want to kill us?"

"No doubt about it," said Lewis. "Henry Gray is an honest man, and he is telling the truth. It's bad, Will. I have James and Thomas loading a wagon. I am giving you two of my fastest horses. We will go over there now and put these things into the wagon, and you can be off."

Dent came to life just as Lewis lifted him up into the wagon. "I want my dog." he said. "Can he go too?"

"Good idea," said Will, and he whistled for Toby who came around the house.

"Up in the wagon Toby," said Lewis.

Lydia brought the frightened children in to the living room, and had barely time to gather some diapers and blankets. She urged Martha to put on her shoes and get a coat. She had hurriedly put some food and tin cups into a pillow case and got her shawl from the peg.

Will finally saw the danger. "I will leave Lydia and the children with you, Lewis, and come for them later."

"Oh no, Will," said Lydia, "we are all going. My children will not be safe here."

"Hang a bucket and a tub on the wagon, Lewis, while I get the family in the wagon. We will need them camping on the way. Oh, and an ax and hammer."

Lewis said, "Thomas is doing all that on my wagon. Now hurry." Lydia lay George down beside Martha and told her to cover him up and she held John on her lap on the wagon seat. As Will climbed up into the wagon, Lewis threw his coat up to the children. "Just in case you need it, Will," he said.

Lydia wrapped her shawl around John.

"Here, Will, is some money," and he shoved a roll of bills into his hands. "Don't worry about the farm. I will take care of everything. Write me from your brother's or wherever you're going, and give me an address to contact you. Rafe won't know which direction you have gone, and you will have at least three hours head start. I will go and get

21

a horse and tell the man at the carriage house to leave for a couple of days. Now get going, and don't waste any time. Dent, you and Martha lie down on those quilts and go back to sleep. Everything will be all right. Don't worry, and be good."

Will looked up and saw Thomas and James pulling the wagon into his yard. They transferred all the things into Lewis' wagon and put the children in. Lydia covered them with a quilt. Will said, "Thanks for everything," to Thomas and James. "Lewis, I owe you."

Will drove out into the road and headed north, and Lydia looked back at her brothers and her father, and wondered when she would ever see them again.

## Chapter
# FIVE

The night was dark except for the moonlight as they left Elyton behind. Will said nothing for a long time. He seemed deep in thought. Lydia had her own thoughts. She pulled her shawl around her shoulders. She loved Will and trusted him. She knew she would go anywhere with him.

The children were quiet now after the sobbing ceased, and she hoped they had gone to sleep.

Up through Tennessee they traveled. They stopped at creeks to water the horses. When there was no more light, Will pulled off the road. "We will have to wait until dawn to go any farther," he said. "Can you sleep a little back there with Dent and Martha? I'll get down and help you."

Will checked to see if he could get farther off the road. He wanted the wagon to be safe. He walked a little and saw the ground was solid, so he decided that would be best. He thought it wouldn't be long until daylight now. He put his gun beside him. He put Toby on the floor near his feet. He knew Toby would bark at the sight of anyone stopping, and warn them of danger. He lay on the wagon seat and pulled Lewis' coat over his lap. "God, keep us," he said out loud.

Will was awake with the first rays of light. He started up the wagon and proceeded down the road. He was stiff from sleeping in a cramped position on the wagon seat. Lydia woke with the motion of the wagon and sat up. Little George whimpered, and John began to cry. He needed changing. Will said to her. "I'll find a place to pull off and camp now that it is getting light. Try to find something they can nibble on."

Dent said, "I can reach the basket, Mama," and he handed it to her. The biscuits were hard and cold apples were refused. Then she found some fried apple pies wrapped in cloth napkins, enough for each of them to have one. It kept them quiet for a while.

Soon the light from the rising sun gave Will more vision and he saw a road leading off so he turned into it. Soon he saw a clearing. Dent called. "Papa, there's a place."

"I see it, Son," he answered. "There is a nice stream there too." The children watched with interest as their father stopped the wagon and got down.

"All right, you little fellows, let's get into some dry clothing. Lydia, is there anything left they can eat? If we can build a fire, I can heat us some coffee. Anna has packed some ham. We will take the skillet and heat it up and soak the biscuits in coffee. We'll make do until I can find a store to get milk, or to a house where they will sell us some."

While Dent got water from the stream, Will led the horses down so they could drink. He got some oats out for them and then turned to Lydia, "Let's get some stones and make a little fireplace here. Dent, see if you can find the coffee pot and the skillet." said Will.

Lydia said, "It is in the blue basket, Dent. I will hand it down. I have to get dry clothes for John. Take George out to the woods there, and tell him to be good. Lydia was quick to change John, and Dent found more dry wood for the fire. The quilts would get wet on the dewy ground but Lydia didn't have any other choice. She spread them out, and Martha and Dent sat down holding the little boys. Will came back and helped Lydia with the ham and the coffee. Lydia said, "I will go get the cups. I know where they are."

"I'll let the horses rest a bit, and then I will go down the road a ways and see if there is a settlement. I won't take the wagon, just one of the horses."

"This is a pretty place, Mama," said Dent. "I bet there is fish in that stream, and things to eat in the woods."

"I know you have read such things in books, Dent, but we don't have time to search like that. Do you want to try a little biscuit soaked in coffee? I don't approve of your drinking it, but this is a have-to case."

Martha said, "I want some too, Mama. The ham smells so good."

They drank water from the stream and lay on their quilts. Will put a saddle on Jonah and said, "Dent, look after your mother. I won't be long."

"We will clean up everything, so we can leave when Papa gets back. I will wash out these diapers and put them in a pillow case. At least we can have them later on. We want to get to your Grandpa's as fast as we can."

"Tell us about Grandpa, Mama."

"I haven't met him, Dent. Will says he is a fine man, and his brothers are too.

Dent dried the cups and put the coffee pot back in the wagon. Lydia had already washed the pan, and they stayed there near the fire until Will came riding back.

"There is a little store down that road, Lydia. We will get going and hope that is open by the time we get down there. It is early yet."

Lydia felt much better hearing the news. When the sun was overhead, they were well up into Tennessee. With the supplies from the store they were satisfied, and the children drank their milk. "We will finish it, Lydia," said Will, "because it will spoil easily."

The trees were lush with green leaves, and there were sounds of birds everywhere. It was a pleasant drive, and the road climbed and dipped. Lydia said, "Will, it is beautiful."

"Yes," he answered. "I love the Tennessee land. My father wanted to buy down in Roane County where the soil was rich and it was selling cheap. He has built up a good homestead there now. I know you will like my father and mother, Lydia. They are good people."

They drove on until Will needed to rest the horses. After a short stop in a field with a clear running creek, they drank water and had sandwiches and fruit. Once more John was changed, and Lydia said she would throw away the diapers, because she didn't care to wash them, and they would buy more. Soon they were on their way again. Lydia had laid their quilts where the sunshine would hit them in the wagon and they would dry. Will told Martha and Dent to watch for a road turning off on either side of the main road. It would occupy them, he thought for a while.

As they drove along, the road became steeper. George sat between Lydia and Will. She talked to him, and he was quiet. Will told them about his home in Scott County when he was a boy and the hours flew by. Lydia said, "Will, tell us about your mother and father."

"You will like them, Lydia," he said. "They left Scott when land went for sale cheap in Roane County. Before long my brothers Jesse and Hugh went down and also bought land. My mother has other grandchildren besides you and Dent, Martha," and he turned to smile at her. Will began to tire and asked Dent to keep looking for a campsite or signs of a town on the road.

After a while Dent said, "I see one Pa, up on the right."

Martha said, "I see the water through the trees."

"Down a little lane right through those trees, Pa," said Dent.

Will turned down the sloping road he felt a wobbly movement of one wagon wheel.

"I think we are losing a wheel," he said. "I'll have to pull over and see."

He examined the wheel and told Dent and Lydia that it was coming loose, and he would lead the horses down the little lane where they could rest.

"We will have to stop at the first place we can turn off," he said.

"It is private land but maybe I can explain if anyone comes along. No fires Dent. I will saddle Jonah and ride along this road and try to find a wheelwright. I better leave some of this money in the wagon, Lydia, and there is a loaded gun under the wagon seat. I don't expect any trouble, but just so you know. Dent, I expect you to look after your mother."

"I will," said Dent. Will disappeared around the bend of the road. Lydia got the quilts out of the wagon and the rest of the food and the cups for water. Dent took George and John to walk a little and keep them quiet, while Lydia and Martha cleaned up around the camp. Both George and John were asleep on the quilts when Will appeared with another rider who was carrying a new wagon wheel.

"This is Winston Terry," he said to Lydia. "My wife, Lydia."

"We will get right to work, Mr. Wilson. Between us, we will have this changed in no time. Right around the bend is where Mrs. Landry lives. If you want to drive down there she can sell you some milk for your children. She's is a very nice lady and wouldn't mind helping." He shouldered the used wheel and rode off waving to them.

"I went straight to the right place," said Will. "He was nice to ride back with me to save me a trip."

After a quick stop at Mrs. Landry's house where they bought milk, bread and an apple pie, they hurried on.

For hours they drove with short breaks for the horses to rest and drink from a stream.

Will was tired and his arms ached. He considered pulling off to camp, but decided to keep going. He stopped at a creek and told Lydia to change the baby, and get them settled for the night. They drank thirstily and ate a luscious pear each and washed their hands in the stream.

After Will rested, he said to Lydia, "We still have two more days before we get to Kingston. With this wagon trouble, it set me to thinking. I think we should sell the wagon and team in the next town and get railway tickets to Kingston. We can buy a trunk for our things and ship it on.

"I can't get on a train in these smelly, dirty clothes, and the children are dirty, too."

"Then we will spend the night in an inn, and I will go buy some new clothes. Lewis gave me enough money to do that with plenty left over."

Will checked his family in at the Wildwood Inn in Woodby, Tennessee. He asked for water to be sent up so they could bathe. Will took the team and wagon to the barn behind the inn and spoke to the attendant about a possible sale.

"Look after the things in the wagon," he said, as he left the man. "I will see you in the morning".

"I am Christopher Smith," said the young man. "I am pretty sure the owner would be interested in buying the wagon and team."

Will left Lydia asleep the following morning and went down to breakfast. He then went to a general store and bought clothes for everyone and railway tickets to Kingston.

Returning to the inn, he talked to the owner, Mr. Huddleston, and was offered a fair price for the wagon and team. "I will give you $100 extra for all that is in the wagon, too," he said.

As the train climbed higher, Lydia watched from her window. It was getting colder. The March winds blew harder and the trees swayed and bent. Lydia said to Will. "If we get settled somewhere, will you still have time to plant a garden?"

"Yes, it depends on where we can afford to buy. It will take Lewis some time to sell our stock and the land. I can send him power of attorney as soon as I can manage it. We will go to Papa's first in Roane County."

"Where in Roane County?"

"It is about 10 miles southwest of Kingston, the county seat. My twin brother, Jesse lives close to him too. We will see them all."

"I hope it isn't too much on your parents to have us all visit."

"They will love it, Lydia. I have been promising them for months that we would come."


In Roane County, William Wilson and his wife, Jane, were sleeping. William jumped up and said to Jane. "I hear something. It sounds like harness jingling." Then he heard his two hunting dogs barking in the front yard. He rushed to the window and saw a lantern. A wagon was nearing his house.

William stepped out on his porch. There it was coming into his lane. He went in and lit a lamp and carried it back outside.

"Hey, Papa," he heard, "It's me, Will. Make those dogs quiet down."

Will climbed from the wagon and grabbed his father in a bear hug. "What on earth, Will?" he said. "In the middle of the night? What's wrong, Son?" Jane was awakened by the barking dogs, and stepped out on the porch. "It's Will, Janie," he said. Will went hugged his mother.

"My whole family is in this wagon. Ma, do you think there's room for all of us to bed down?"

"We will make room," said Jane happily. "Light some more lamps William, and let's get those children out of that wagon bed. Oh, the poor little mites."

As Will helped Lydia down he told William, "This is my wife, Papa. Meet Lydia."

"Well, you sure look tuckered out. We will get you inside right away." Jane made pallets on the floor for Dent and Martha. She told them to go right to sleep and they would talk in the morning. She then made up a big bed for Will and Lydia, and said, "Can you sleep with the little boys just for tonight? This is the only extra bed I have. We will get another tomorrow."

"Of course," answered Will.

"Just put them in like they are. These sheets can be washed," said Jane "I'll put on some coffee as soon as the stove heats up." Will tucked George and John in, and followed Jane out to the kitchen. William came in the back door having taken the horses to the barn and given them oats and water.

The coffee was ready and William took a cup and sat at the table. "Now, Son, tell me about this trip." After the story had been explained, and Lydia was drooping, Jane said, "It is good to have you all here Lydia. You go on into the bedroom, and I will get one of my nightgowns, and a nightshirt for Will. You need to get some sleep, and William and I will go back to bed too."

Will said, "I will need to take the rented wagon back to the station master tomorrow."

## Chapter
# SIX

Dent woke up on the pallet on the floor. He turned and saw Martha nearby on another. He saw a huge fireplace all clean and shiny. There were chairs with bright covers. "Wake up Martha. We're at Grandma's house!"

Martha joined him at the window. "Oh look, Dent. Morning glories! Hundreds of them. They are so pretty. Let's go outside."

Lydia awoke and looked around. She was in a bed. A real bed! "Wake up, Will!" she said, "John has soaked me and probably George too. We'll have to wash all this bedding and apologize to your mother."

Will looked over at her. His whiskers made him look old, and his father's nightshirt made Lydia start laughing. "Never mind," he said. "We can buy Ma a whole new bed." He walked to the window. "Will you look at that?" he said. "Dent and Martha are out there playing with Pa's dog. I will go see if Ma is up. Can you imagine what she thought when we all piled in?" and he laughed.

"She seemed pleased to me. She had her boy home and her grandchildren, too."

Jane was up and had a fire going in her cook stove.

"Sit down," she said, "there will be coffee ready in a few minutes."

William came through the kitchen door. "I'll go milk and feed. Want to come, Dent?"

"Yes," said Dent, and he jumped up right away.

Lydia came in carrying John, and sat at the table.

Jane poured Will a cup of coffee. "The biscuits will be done in a few minutes," she said.

After a huge meal of hot biscuits, ham, and cream gravy, they were all satisfied, and William asked his son if he would like to take a look at the farm. George had turned over his milk and Lydia was mopping it up. Martha went to wash her hands where the milk had spattered on her. "Whatever will Grandma think of us?" said Lydia.

Jane said, "I have raised three sons. I have seen many a spill," and laughed merrily.

"Jane, I am so sorry about your bed. I am afraid John has soaked it. Will and I must go into town and buy you another mattress. And I will wash all the bedding".

"Never mind that. We will put it outside in the sun, and I'll put some lye soap to it. It will be as good as new."

"Will got us a few things to wear in Woodby, but we will need to do some shopping. My father gave us money before we left, so we are all right until Father sells some of the stock for us. It is real nice to finally get here and get some decent rest, and I am glad you could take us in for a few days," Lydia hugged her mother - in - law again.

"I am just happy to have you and to see my grandchildren. I am so happy to meet my daughter-in-law, too," said Jane. "We'll have a nice long visit and make up for all those years."

Will and his father rode horses to the border line of his property on the north side.

"This is beautiful country, Pa," he said. "You ought to be proud."

"I have done pretty well here," he said, "The ground is more fertile here than in Scott, and less hilly, easier to plow, and cultivate crops. There's room to spread out here. The climate suits us."

"I can see Ma is looking well," agreed Will.

"Yes, she is very happy here."

"But don't you miss the mountains?"

"There are enough mountains around here to suit me. If I want to go hunting or fishing, I do. I can always go back and visit Scott whenever I want to."

"Let's head back, and I'll help Lydia with the children. She has been wonderful, Papa, leaving her family like that, and enduring the long trip up here. I hope I can repay her someday for all that."

"I understand, Will. It was the same with your Ma. We left North Carolina the same way although in not so much of a hurry. She left her family there, too, and I think she has had no regrets. By the way, let's go see what she is planning for dinner. I can expect it will be a big one. Son, that woman is happier than I have seen her in a long time."

Lydia had been talking to Jane as they bathed the children, and found things for them to wear.

"Jesse's kids are always leaving something over here." She found clothes that fit all the children.

Lydia said, "Oh, Jane, it is so good of you to put us up like this. Whatever is going to happen to us?" And to her dismay started to cry. Instantly Jane's arms were around her while she murmured words of encouragement.

"Never you mind. Will is a smart boy. He will take care of everything."

Lydia dried her eyes and put on a smile.

"There they come now. Let's just have more coffee while they decide what to do today."

While Jane was cooking, William took Will and the children down to his son Jesse's place. While Will visited with Jesse and his wife, Susan, William took a horse and rode to Hugh's farm to tell them that Will and Lydia were in Roane County at his house for a while. When he rode back,

Hugh was with him and ran to see his brother. William was carrying a large sack on the back of his horse. Hugh's wife, Jan, had sent some things to Lydia.

"Let's all ride back to eat. I know Ma is cooking up a bunch of things, and she will expect Jesse and Hugh to come and eat."

"Me, too," said Jesse's wife. And they all merrily set off for William's house.

Will had looked for several days around Roane County for property to buy. Time was passing.

One evening he said, "Pa, I think Lydia and I will go up to Scott County. Would you mind if we leave George and John here for a few days. We will take Martha and Dent with us."

Jane said, "Of course you must leave them here. I know I am not going to have them forever. I want to spend time with them."

"Lydia, can you and the children be ready on Friday morning early? Pack a hamper of food, and carry bedding and wraps. It may be cold at night."

The road climbed into the forests and through the mining towns. Lydia watched with interest. "It is so rugged, but very beautiful," she said.

"I must be very careful. Some of these places are steep and dangerous."

When they got to New River, they got a room at the inn. The stable behind the building housed the horses and stored the wagon. The food was very good, and they ate heartily. Will had extra coffee. Will led his family upstairs to get a good night's rest.

Morning came before Martha and Dent wanted to get up, but they were coaxed out of the bed and got ready to leave. They breakfasted in the dining room, and Will left to see about the wagon and team. They paid their bill, and went on their way to Norma, a little village in the foothills of Brimstone Mountain in Scott County.

It was a pleasant drive through the valleys and going up the little rises. They drove on till mid-morning and then pulled off the road to rest the animals and stretch their legs. They ate a snack and drank from a creek, where the horses drank their fill. It flowed cold down the hill at a fast speed.

After another few hours, they arrived in Norma. They passed the Norma Baptist Church. Will showed Lydia the places he recognized. "I think I see a familiar name," he said. The sign read, "Luther Harness. "General Store and Norma Post Office."

Dent and Martha were still asleep, so they left them in the wagon. As they walked in, they were greeted by Luther who shook Will's hand, and Will introduced Lydia to Luther.

"We were old school chums."

"Doing good down there in Alabama?" he asked.

"That is debatable, Luther," answered Will. They walked over to the cracker barrel and bought a few crackers and some cheese and fruit.

"I am looking for some property, Luther. Do you know of any for sale?"

"Well, Let me think," said Luther. "There's the old Rhymes place near the Jamestown Road. It would go cheap. I heard old Elmer Creech had his farm up for sale. He can't farm anymore and moved in with his daughter and son-in-law. Now that is a real nice place. It has a house on it, and I know of two springs on the property."

"We are kind of on a tight schedule, Luther. Do you think we could talk to this Mr. Creech today?"

"Sure. I will just write down the directions for you. They are west off the Jamestown Road. How are your folks, Will?"

"Just fine. They are in Roane County now. So are my brothers."

Will shook hands with Luther, and said, "Goodbye. We will be back in later."

Lydia and Will drove down past the Mill road, and he showed Lydia some of the places he knew. They stopped at a small stream and ate their cheese and crackers and drank from the stream. Soon they were on their way again.

They found Mr. Creech sitting on the front porch and pulled into the yard. Mr. Creech stood up, and his wife came out on the porch. Will introduced himself and Lydia. "Come on up and sit," said Mr. Creech. "This is my wife, Maggie. Honey, why don't you get us some apple cider to drink?"

Will came right to the point. "Mr. Creech, I hear you have a farm to sell. I am from this area, and I want to come back for a while. I am interested." They talked and the cider was brought. Mr. Creech's daughter, Lenora, came out and sat in a rocker. She smiled shyly at Lydia.

"I do have some nice acreage over to the east. I lived for years on that piece of land. Do you want to ride out and see it?"

"I do," said Will.

Mr. Creech rose, and turned to his daughter. "Get my hat." Then he walked down to the buggy in the yard. "Nothing like the present," he said.

"I couldn't agree more," said Will with a laugh.

The property was just what Will had in mind. Some of it was fields and some forest. They rode over it and looked at the log and frame house. Lydia was so impressed with the five rooms with their high ceilings, and the huge fireplace in the parlor. It had two large porches. She hoped Will would make a bargain with Mr. Creech.

When they drove back to Elmer Creech's house his wife, Maggie, had a basket of apples for Dent and Martha. "I put in a jar of blackberry preserves for your mother-in-law, Lydia. If you decide to live here, we will be happy to have you as a new neighbor, so be sure to let us know. We will be happy to help you settle in."

Will said to Lydia, "It is too late to start back today. Darkness would catch us before got to New River. We'll ride out to the property and have a snack there. We'll look around some more. I have told Elmer Creech that we will take it. He will have the papers drawn up. We will eat supper and stay in the inn tonight."

Lydia and Martha peeked in the windows of the house, and Will and Dent looked at the spring house again. They scooped up a drink from the cold water. They ate apples, crackers and cheese on the steps of the porch. "It is a beautiful piece of land, Will," said Lydia. "I think we will be happy here."

At the inn in town, they checked in, and Will took care of the horses and wagon. Lydia, Martha and Dent went upstairs to their room. Will asked the keeper if he would send up some hot water and towels, and he nodded. They washed up and went down to supper. They enjoyed fried trout, potatoes, and bread and butter. Dent said he wanted to go right to bed so he would be ready to go by dawn. Soon he and Martha were sound asleep. Will and Lydia talked quietly for a few minutes and Lydia nodded off. He smiled down at her and whispered, "Dream on, my darling. You are going to be in your own place with all your children around you really soon."

The following morning they were on their way again with a packaged lunch made by the cook for their snack on the road. As they rounded the first curve, Dent said, "I feel a lot better this morning, Papa. I wish we could drive straight through to Grandpa's."

"Well, Son, I am afraid we can't do that. I would like to as well. We will just have to be patient."

The morning was dewy and fresh, and they made good time going on a downward slant toward New River. The lush greenery gave out a pine scent and other smells that Lydia didn't recognize. She saw morning glories open everywhere she looked. The day became warmer and she shed her wrap.

"I see a good place to rest the horses," said Will. He pulled down into a cedar grove and unhitched the horses so they could move about. There was a spring, so Will took a bucket from the wagon and filled it with water for the horses.

Lydia took two quilts from the back of the wagon, and they sat down. She admired the peaceful little glen. "We'll eat our lunch here and be on our way," said Will. The food was delicious. "I have a good feeling, children that we are going to be very satisfied in the new place.

"How about you?" Both agreed and wanted to get back to it as soon as possible.

Will turned in the lane to William's house and told Lydia, "Go on in. I will take the horses to the stable and see to them."

When he returned, Lydia met him at the door. "George and John are already asleep," she said. "Jane and William are in the parlor."

Will took a seat near his mother with Lydia beside him, and Dent and Martha sat at his feet.

"Papa," he began, "we found the place we wanted. A good stand of trees, hardwoods and others, and the place has a farmhouse and a spring house all ready to use."

"How much land?"

"Fifty acres in all, some good looking fields, and there is water on the property. I am very satisfied with the price, and Lydia agrees with me."

Lydia said, "Jane, there is a five room house with two large porches, front and back, and a little pantry off the kitchen. The people who lived there said it was a well-built house, and they only left because Mr. Creech was not able to farm anymore."

"It just sounds wonderful," answered Jane. "I know the children will love it."

"We met some good people who will be our neighbors. One of them is Evie and her husband, Earl Brown. She cleans the church, and she is a very nice lady. You remember Luther Harness? He has a general store, and he and his wife run the post office."

William said, "Yes, I remember him well, and his father too."

Just then Lydia yawned and he glanced at her affectionately.

Will said, "Now, children, you should get to bed. We need to rest and there is plenty to do tomorrow. Just be thinking about packing your new clothes and gifts, for we will be going back fairly soon."

Martha and Dent hugged their parents, and went straight to their beds, and Will sighed.

"Were John and George much trouble?" asked Will.

"No, indeed, they were very well behaved, and I adore them. I will be sorry to see them go. Can you bring them back to see me real soon?"

"Well, I am sure that can be arranged. Let's all turn in," said William. "We have a big day of plans tomorrow."

# Chapter
# SEVEN

For the next few days, Will and Lydia packed quilts, homespun sheets, and towels were set aside to wrap breakable things. Dishes and pots were put into the barrels, and the children's clothes were all stacked ready to be placed in the barrels.

"We will take only necessary things. We can manage until we come back to see you folks again."

Will and his father discussed what tools were needed from the shed, since the wagon would only hold so much.

"I've been thinking, Will," said William. "Since you and Lydia will be so busy getting settled, why not think of leaving George and John here until you come back for more things. We would love to have them, and it won't be so hard on Jane for all of them to go at once. Do you think Lydia would agree?"

"It sounds like a great idea to me. We can only ask her. Maybe Ma can get her to come around."

At supper Jane brought up the subject. Lydia was tired, and she said right away, "I don't know if I can do without my babies. I appreciate it, Jane. I haven't been away from them very much."

Jane said, "At least think about it. You can come for them any time. and things would go so much faster for you and Will if you didn't need to attend to two little boys."

"I will," said Lydia, "I will give it some thought."

Lydia was scrubbing out diapers in the back yard when Jane came out. She stopped and wiped her forehead. "It sure is warm to day."

"I brought you some cold water. Let's sit a minute," answered Jane.

"I have been thinking about what you said, Jane. It will really be hard on George and John at first. We don't even have beds yet."

"That is true," said Jane. "Just leave them here. I can't stand to see them all go at once. I'll take good care of them for you. You just come back when you're ready, and we will fix them a big bunch of clothes and things, so it will be easier for you."

"I'll talk to Will," said Lydia. "I promise."

The Wilsons set out at dawn in the loaded wagon. Dent and Martha sat behind their parents in wooden chairs their grandfather had made for them. Lydia, at first, was sorry she had left George and John behind, but common sense took over, and she knew it was best. Little George was promised a chair of his own if he would be good, when Jane had put them to bed.

They had worked tirelessly packing the wagon, and William had hung a washtub and scrub board on the side, plus a broom and mop.

Lydia was so excited to be going to her own home, nothing like the one she left in Alabama, but she longed to have her brood around her again in their own house. She was anxious to get there and get it ready.

Jane had packed a basket of food, hot flaky biscuits stuffed with ham. Lydia had wrapped a gallon jar of milk in homespun towels, for them to drink when they stopped to rest. They would find a place to pull off the road to Scott County.

"Will, the road is even prettier than we saw it before. The mountains are greener, and the breeze is heavenly."

"Well, Dent, it looks like you and Martha will be going to school in Scott County in the fall." He turned and smiled at his children.

Before the sun was over head, Will turned the wagon off on a little dirt road and found a stream with beeches and a huge weeping willow for shade. He helped everyone down and took his horses to drink in the stream. Lydia spread a quilt on the grass, and soon they were enjoying the delicious biscuits and ham, and drinking the milk from tin cups. After a few minutes of rest, Will said, "We need to move on so we can get to New River before dark."

Lydia washed the cups and Will packed up the quilt. Dent and Martha wanted him to hang the chairs on the other side of the wagon so they could stretch out and nap. They had left before they were fully awake, and now they wanted to doze.

On and on they drove enjoying the scenery until they reached New River, a pretty little settlement with stores, church, post office and other buildings. The children woke and looked around. Will said, "We'll spend the night in the inn up there."

He hitched the horses to the rail, and they immediately drank from the water trough. Will went inside to rent a room.

When he returned, he helped Lydia and the children to the ground and gave Lydia the key. "Go on up, and I will take the team around to the livery in back."

He spoke to the attendant, and asked him to put the wagon in a safe place, and he took one bag from it and carried it to the inn.

He went inside and asked for hot water to be sent up and then mounted the stairs.

All clean and refreshed, Will took his family to the dining room where they ate a delicious meal. The children drank milk, while Lydia and Will had tea.

They were all ready for a night of rest as soon as they reached their room once more.

At last they turned onto the road to Norma. They passed the church, and saw Evie out in the church yard with a bucket and broom. Will pulled over and stopped.

"Oh, Will, I am so glad to see you back," she said.

"Yes. We have finally arrived."

Lydia said, "Hello" to Evie.

"How was the trip?"

"Without a problem," said Lydia.

Will said, "Goodbye," and they started to go.

Evie called to them. "Don't bother about supper. We will be over to bring some fried chicken and biscuits for you. Earl will be so glad you made it safely."

Will tied the horses to a tree, and found a pan to put water for them. Then he began to unpack the wagon. Soon they all sat to rest, drinking cool water from the spring. "So much to do, Will," Lydia said.

"Yes, we need to prepare the pallets before dark. Dent can put the chairs inside."

"Martha and I will take care of the food. We will have to cook over the fireplace for a while. But that will be fun, won't it?"

As they finished putting the things Jane had packed for them on the shelves, Dent took feed for the horses.

"We will have to fix a place for them," said Will. "I will go tomorrow to the store and get some wire, just enough for a small enclosure. Later we will need to build a barn."

Will and Lydia had sat down on the steps to rest a few minutes when they saw Evie and Earl turning off in the lane toward the house. Will shook hands with Earl.

"Welcome, home, Will," he said. "Glad you made it. Evie and I brought your first meal in your new place, even plates and forks in case you haven't unpacked yet. Evie hugged Lydia and spoke to the children.

"You have a fine family," she said.

"Thanks," said Lydia.

"I hope you are hungry."

Dent said, "We are!" They all laughed at him. They sat on the steps, and Dent and Martha in the two little chairs, and ate the fried chicken and biscuits. Some were stuffed with blackberry jelly. "This so nice of you," said Will. "We can wait until tomorrow now to dig out the skillet and things."

"Just glad to do it," said Evie.

That night the Wilsons sought their pallets almost at sundown. They were ready to sleep and get up early to face a new day and explore the grounds.


Will was brewing coffee in a scarred pot on the fire. "I don't know whether to make a table first or a bench," he said. Will and Lydia sat in the two chairs, and Dent and Martha took their plates and sat on the front steps.

Wild flowers grew around the yard and toward the fields. "They are so pretty." remarked Martha.

"I'm going back for more eggs," said Dent, "Want some?"

"I'm stuffed," said Martha. "I want some water though." Lydia piled the rest of the eggs on Will's and Dent's plates, and they sat drinking coffee and planning the day.

"We have plenty to do today," said Lydia.

"Yes. That's true. First off, I am going to take the wagon into town. I'll get some wire and lumber for posts to build a little place for the horses so they can move about. Later I'll make a rail fence for a wider area. I'll get more supplies. I'll also go see Freeman at the bank and open an account. We need a cow and some chickens. We need milk and eggs for the children. I will check in Norma for someone who might have some stock to sell."

Dent wanted to go too, but Will said, "Not this time, Son. I need you to stay and help your mother. I am depending on you to take good care of her and your sister. When I get back you can help me with the fence. There will plenty of times you can go with me."

Lydia got out her zinc wash tub and some lye soap. "We'll clean this place up while you're gone," she said. "Be sure to ask the store clerk about ordering things. Find out about a post office, too. We will want to write home and let them know about the new place." She watched as Will drove the wagon out to the road. He turned back to wave at the little family.

Lydia said, "Well, Dent and Martha. What do you think of our new home?"

Both children danced around her merrily. "I think it is the best spot in the whole world," said Martha. Dent said, "Mama, it is so big. I want to go and look at all the grounds again when you don't need me anymore."

The day flew by. Lydia and the children stayed very busy. They finally saw Will coming into view and he yelled greetings from the road. It was so good to see his family in the yard and his house behind them. He figured his happiness could boil right over.

"Hope you've got some coffee, Lyddie," he said. "I could sure use some. He hugged her, and rolled up his sleeves. He sat on the steps and drank the coffee and looked at the trees, and the mountains rising up in the distance. "I got the account opened," he said.

Lydia poured a cup of coffee for herself and sat beside him.

"We got a lot done today. We scrubbed all the rooms and washed clothes. Dent helped with the iron pot and we hung some things on the porch railings."

"I'll put you up a clothes line as soon as I can. I need to fix a place for the horses first. Dent, do you want to help me with that?"

Dent agreed. He wanted to get started right away.

"First let's bring in the things that I bought in town. I'll carry the can of lard, and you and Martha can bring the baskets of food. Toby ran around barking.

"He wants to play," said Dent. "We don't have time, Toby. We have work to do."

Martha and Lydia put up supplies on the pantry shelves. Dent and Will took the wire from the wagon, and carried the tools from the back porch. Will brought the lumber he had bought. He made posts and stretched the wire until it covered a wide space, and made a makeshift gate. When the horses were placed inside, they put water pans and food in the enclosure.

"That will do until we can start on the barn," said Will.

"Will that be tomorrow?" asked Dent.

"No, Son, I need to get the garden plowed first, and get a crop in. We are late already."

Dent said, "I can help you put in the crop, can't I?"

"You sure can. We'll do it together."

It was cool that day. The weather seemed to change abruptly. Mocking birds and thrush were building nests, and squirrels were chattering in the trees. "I like this place, Papa," said Dent.

They went back to the house after getting fresh water from the spring. As they rested, Lydia asked Will if he learned about furniture and things they would need.

"Yes," he answered. "There are carpenters here who make furniture. There is a saw mill where all kinds of lumber can be bought. Luther said there are traders that come through twice a month, and will take orders for merchandise, and bring it back on their next trip. They bring all kinds of things to sell to Mr. Harness, and then we buy from him, and tell him what we need to order. I got some paper and stamps for you, and I sent off a short note to Lewis and to Pa and Ma and put them in the mail."

"I'll write them when I have a chance." said Lydia. "There's some supper by the fire. I will be glad to get my stove up from Roane so I can do a better job of cooking."

"What a day!" he said. "One night of rest and I will go to the saw mill for lumber. I plan to make some temporary beds for us. They will do until our new ones arrive."

"I am so tired I could sleep anywhere," said Lydia with a laugh. "I got everything I could think of to make our pallets softer. The sun lowered over the trees and blackness descended on the little group and they gladly sought their beds.

The next morning, Will and Lydia awoke to shouts outside, and the sounds of horses and wagons. They jumped up, and Lydia threw on her robe over her nightgown, and Will grabbed for his trousers. Lydia handed him a shirt from a peg on the wall, just as another shout came from outside. "Wilsons, are you up?" Lydia threw open the door to find the yard full of people she had never seen before.

Will saw Elmer Creech getting down from a wagon, and then helping his wife, Maggie, to alight. "We came to get your garden plowed," he said. More wagons came into the yard. "These are my nephews and their sons."

His son-in-law, Frank Jeffers, carried two fat hens, their legs tied together. "All right if I just throw these in with the horses?" He untied them and pitched them over the fence.

Mrs. Creech followed him to the porch. "I brought corn for the chickens," she said.

Lydia greeted them joyously, and Will slapped Frank on the back.

"It sure is good of you to do this," he said. "I was planning to get to the garden next." Mr. Creech and a blond haired young man were getting the plow from one of the wagons.

"This is my cousin, Henry. Say 'Hello' to Will Wilson, Henry. If you'll tell us which patch you want us to start with, Will, we'll get right to it. How about we start where I had my vegetable garden?" he asked. When the men left to plow, Maggie Creech introduced Naomi, Henry's wife to Lydia.

"We'll just go into the back room and change," said Will.

Lydia said, "I am sorry there are only two chairs right now.

And they are small. Will's father made them for the children."

That is why we came," said Naomi, "to see what you need most."

When Lydia came back dressed in a white calico dress with blue dots, she said, "It is so nice having company."

"What can we do?" asked Mrs. Creech.

"I don't see a stove," said Naomi.

Dent and Martha came in all dressed, for they had heard the men arrive. "My father shipped my stove up to Roane County. We haven't got it here yet. I have a barrel of dishes, silverware and utensils that I haven't unpacked. Will hasn't had time yet to make a place for them."

Another couple came up on to the porch.

"I am happy you came," said Lydia. "I know my husband will be glad to see you. He is out there with the others."

Evie said, "Why don't you just tell Earl what you need the most, and he can be figuring the cost and Mr. Wilson can tell him if it is agreeable. If he wants, Earl can do the work. Earl makes furniture for a living."

"That is a good idea," said Lydia. "I am sure we can do business. I need a dining table and chairs and a work table for the kitchen. We have beds ordered. Mr. Harness said they would arrive soon."

"I brought a couple of quilts," said Evie, shyly. "I hope you can use them."

Mrs. Creech said to Earl, "Will you please go out to our wagon and bring in that pot of chicken and dumplings?"

Lydia could not believe the generosity of these mountain people. Her neighbors in Alabama were nice, but nothing like these friends.

Evie said, "I brought a pot of mashed potatoes and some cornbread. When the men want to rest, we will have it ready for them."

Mrs. Creech said, "Now, Lydia, don't be embarrassed. We like helping our neighbors in Scott. When someone has a barn raising or a gathering, we always bring plenty of food."

"I am sure I will get used to it, and I'll be returning the favors," and she laughed heartily.

"Dent, I see your father coming. Henry has taken over the plow. Go get us some fresh water from the spring. They will be thirsty."

Martha brought water glasses from the barrel and rinsed them out.

"Does the spring need cleaning, Will?" Mrs. Creech asked as Will came in from the porch. "It's been a while since we lived here."

"Not just yet. It will do for a while," he said.

Evie said to Lydia, "I hope you can get your stove up from Roane County soon."

"When do you plan to go after it?" asked Mrs. Creech.

Will drank deeply of the cold water, and then told Dent to take some out to Mr. Creech and Frank who were sitting out under a tree watching the plowing. He turned to Mrs. Creech and said, "I was going down in a few weeks when I get the planting done. We have two more down there, both boys, George and John, and we want to have things set up here before we bring them."

"I have a little laundry stove stored away that you may borrow. It will come in handy until you get yours up here. Maybe I could get Frank to bring it over today. I think I will just go back with him, as I am getting a little tired."

"I would love to borrow it," said Lydia. "It is so hard to cook over the open fire."

Evie said, "I will call the men in to eat, and we can talk to them about it."

Everyone sat on the porch or in the yard on a quilt eating the good food. Then Mr. Creech said, "I think we ought to get home, Maggie. Earl and the others can stay and work until they want to leave, but it's time we should go."

While Lydia washed up all the glasses and plates in the pan of soapy water, she said, "I never dreamed there were such good people in the mountains. It makes me glad I came to Scott County."

Evie said, "I am awfully glad you did come."

Will was saying goodbye to Mr. Creech and thanking him again for all he had done. Frank helped them up to the wagon seat. Mrs. Creech called goodbye to all of them as they left.

Lydia said to Naomi and Evie, "It is time we sat down and had another cup of coffee."

By afternoon the fields had been plowed. They sat down and ate the rest of the chicken and dumplings. Frank returned and brought the laundry heater and several jars of canned tomatoes and pickles.

"These are from Maggie," he said. "She said she canned more than we needed." He and Earl Brown put up the laundry stove and arranged the pipes. Soon a fire was built and fresh coffee was brewing on it. Lydia was delighted with it.

Evie and Earl and the others left, and the Wilson family sat in the yard to rest on the quilt. Lydia said, "I have never met such nice people, Will."

"People around here have always been like that. If they hear of a family that doesn't have enough to eat, they all pitch in. If there is a barn raising or something like this, they want to help."

"Did Earl ask you about the furniture?" asked Lydia.

"Yes, we made a deal, and he will get the lumber he needs and make us a few things. He will bring the work table first."

Will yawned. "And Earl asked me if we planned to buy a cow. I said I did, and he said he knew of a man who had a cow to sell. The man needs the money, so we talked of prices, and he said he would talk to this man about it."

Martha was beginning to nod, so Will said, "I think we should have an early night. I have plenty to do tomorrow, and if I sleep well, I can get up early."

Lydia said, "I think all of us will sleep well tonight."

Dent said as he rose to go inside, "Mama, I got some brush from the woods and put it in for the hens to roost on tonight. I put some water and feed in there, too."

Will said, "That's another job we have, Son. We need to build a hen house! Thank you for thinking of the chickens."

The next morning Will left Lydia fast asleep and went outside. He lit a lantern and walked around, planning where he would put the corn crib, the hen house, and the pig sty. "I think" he said to himself, "I may have to get more help. When the money comes to the bank from Lewis for the sale of the livestock, I'll see about it." He went back and built a fire in the little heater. Lydia joined him and said, "You must be hungry."

"I wanted to get started," he said. "Lydia, you know, I need to get the garden in. One of the men laid off rows in the vegetable garden closest to the house. I need to go in and get seeds and things."

"I have letters to go out," said Lydia.

Martha woke up. Light streaked the eastern sky, and it was a beautiful sight. The fire felt good at first, but soon the heat drove her outside. She walked out and enjoyed seeing the sun come up over the ridges. She went by to pet the horses, and she spotted an egg lying just under the brush that Dent had put there. She reached through the fence and picked it up.

· "I'll tell Papa I found our first egg on the new farm," she said. On the way back she saw the morning glories, so pretty, purple, pink and white, their beautiful trumpet like blossoms opening up. They were climbing up some shrubs that probably had been transplanted by the Creech family.

When she got back to the cabin, Lydia had pancakes made and maple syrup for them. She gave the egg to her mother.

"We don't have any butter for the pancakes, but they will be good anyway," she told Martha. "It won't be long before we have a cow and have our milk and butter again."

Will hitched up the wagon and soon was off to Norma. The day was pleasant, and Will was a very happy person. He had not thought of Alabama in days. "I think Lydia is happy here, too," he thought. He loved her so much for her sacrifice of leaving her family behind to come to a strange place and trust him to take care of her.

At the store, he had a letter from Lewis and Anna. He got the seeds and another hoe and several other things and put them in the wagon. Then he went to the lumber mill. He chose the pieces he wanted and talked to the man there. On the way home, he went by the grist mill and got flour and meal. "I think I have done enough for one day," he said, and started home.

Home. The word sounded good on his tongue. He was born in these mountains and he had come home. The horses trotted along throwing back their heads as if they knew they would not be driven for hours, but would be at home and have food to eat. Will smiled at the thought. He couldn't wait to get there.

## Chapter

# EIGHT

Lydia was very content. She hummed as she worked. There were beds up now for everyone, and she had learned that pots of beans or vegetable soup on the laundry stove saved her a lot of work.

Dent was happy to help his father and enjoyed the praise he received.

Will took them all into town one day, and they stopped to visit Mr. and Mrs. Creech. Lydia got new items at Harness' store. Evie had left some pretty aprons she had made for Lydia and Martha with Mrs. Harness to give to Will when he came in again. Maggie and Lenora were delighted to see them again.

Days went by. The chicken coop was built and Will, Martha and Dent planted seeds. It rained the next day. Will was glad to see the rain. The garden will get a head start, he said."

He walked out to feed the horses and the chickens. The horses were soaked in the falling rain. Will turned to Dent and said, "We need to think seriously of building a barn. The warm rain won't hurt the horses, but by winter we will need to have a shelter up and ready."

The vegetables grew quickly, and Will put in alfalfa for feed and flax for spinning and a few acres of corn. He was glad he didn't have to clear the land before planting.

Will had promised Dent that he could go to town with him, and he would let him drive the team. He took Dent by to see the Creeches and Dent was impressed with the orchards. Mr. Creech's daughter gave him gingerbread and milk, and soon Will said, "We better be on our way. I am going to see Mr. Henley about a sow and a shoat. I heard he wanted me to come by." So they went away with presents for Lydia from Maggie and her daughter, Lenora.

Mr. Henley's place was on the south side of Norma, and Will drove in that direction. He saw Earl driving by and they stopped to chat. "I talked to that man about the cow, Will. He said you could come by and see him." Will got directions and then then went on to Mr. Henley's house. While there, Mrs. Henley was just putting her dinner on the table for her husband and farm hands. She insisted that Will and Dent eat with them. Mr. Henley came in with four young men, who threw their hats in a corner, and sat down at the table. Mrs. Henley told him, "Clem, this is Will Wilson who has come to talk to you about buying a hog. I told him to eat with us first, and then you would talk business."

"Good, sit down, Mr. Wilson, and welcome. How are things with your new place?"

"Coming along nicely," answered Will. "This is my son, Dent." They ate the fine dinner of beef roast and vegetables and cornbread, then Will and Clem went out to see the stock. Dent stayed behind to finish his berry cobbler and milk.

Lydia was tired. She and Martha had worked all day cooking on the laundry stove and scrubbing the wood floors. She longed for the soft carpets at her mother's house. Some day she hoped they would have some rugs too. She sat down to rest with a glass of cold water when she heard Martha calling to her. "I see Papa coming. Come quick!" Lydia went outside. There she saw Will's wagon coming up the road followed by a cow and a calf. She couldn't believe her eyes. Behind them was another wagon driven by two men in overalls and straw hats. Inside their dingy old wagon were two animals. Will called to her, "I got the hog, Lydia. See?"

Mr. Henley and a dark haired man jumped down and said, "Hello, Mrs. Wilson."

Dent said "I'll show you where they go, Mr. Henley," and so the man climbed back up into his wagon and followed Dent to the back of the house and up a little hill. The sty was all ready. Will drove around and untied the cow and calf.

"It is a good milker, Lydia." he said. He led them to the enclosure where the horses were grazing, and opened the gate. "In you go," he said. He grinned at Lydia. "A pretty good days work, wasn't it, Lyddie?" he asked her.

"Oh, Will. Just think! We have milk for our children. It makes me want my babies with us. I hope we can go after them."

"Soon, my dear. We will go get them. I have mail from Papa and Ma here and some from Alabama for you." He hugged Martha who had come up behind Lydia.

"What do you think, little one, he asked?"

"It is just wonderful, Papa," she answered. The calf bawled, and she laughed gleefully. "Isn't it just perfect?" said Lydia.

Will went to see Mr. Henley off with a word of thanks. "Come out and see us when you can and bring your wife."

"Yes, please do," said Lydia.

"Let's go rest, Dent," said his father. "Then we will go feed the hogs and the cow. They need to rest a bit, too, and get used to their new surroundings."

Martha and Dent were up early the next morning, looking at the new stock, and giving their opinions to each other. Dent heard the jingle of harness and turned around. "Look, Martha, there is a wagon turning into our lane!"

Martha shouted, "Ma, Come quick. It's Grandpa and Grandma!"

Will and Lydia came out and ran toward the wagon. There on the front seat with William and Jane were John and George! Lydia began to cry, and Jane got down and hurried to her while William set the little boys down, and they ran to their father. Martha hugged William. "It is so good to see you. Wait till you see our new calf, Grandpa!"

Jane hurried over to give Dent and Martha a hug. "You kids are brown as berries, and you've grown, too."

Everyone went inside the cabin. Lydia sat down with her babies and couldn't say very much. "Lydia we brought you some things."

Will said, "You will have to wait a bit, Papa. She is still in hog heaven!"

Dent said, "We will go get fresh water, Papa. There's some fried pies in the warmer, Martha. Go on and get them while I go to the spring."

Lydia finally stirred herself to serve her company. Jane told them of the things she had brought from Roane County. Sheets and bedding from Jan and Jesse. Canned preserves from Hugh and his wife, and letters to everyone.

William said, "Lydia, I brought you a churn and dashers and a crock for kraut. You haven't bought one yet, have you?"

"No, and I am sure glad you brought them," said Lydia. "We have a cow now, and I will be glad to get to make butter again."

Lydia rose and started for the kitchen. "I better get the stove going and get breakfast. I bet you are all hungry."

"Not after those fried pies," said William, "but no doubt George and John will be ready to eat again by the time breakfast is ready. "Martha, why don't you and Dent show me the cow? We can unload the wagon later."

Will said, "I'll go unhitch your horses and put them in with mine."

After riding around to see the property, William and Jane told Will that it was a beautiful place and thought he had made a good bargain. Jane rested in Lydia's room.

Will told his father that he had ordered the lumber for his barn and he could fell some trees to use also.

"You have made a good start, Son," his father said. "I think you will prosper here, and put the heartbreak of Alabama behind you." Will worked in his field for a few hours, and then helped Dent and William unload the churn and the earthenware crock from the back of the wagon. The packages from Jesse and Hugh were already inside and admired by all.

William said, "I think I will take a rest also, if you don't mind."

Lydia gave him a quilt in case he needed cover, and he went to the bedroom and joined Jane on the big four-poster.

Morning came and Dent was up before the rest. He gathered eggs and fed the chickens. He came in as Lydia was building a fire in the little stove to start breakfast.

"I got the eggs, Ma." he said.

"You're such a help to me, Dent. We may need more wood for the stove. I can't make biscuits, but I can make pancakes and sausages."

Will saw Evie at the store. "Evie, I want you to meet my father. He is William Wilson, Sr. and I am Junior. Papa, this is our good friend, Evie Brown. She has been a great help to me and Lyddie."

"Thank you for that. Will needs friends right now."

"I would like to come out and meet your mother, Will," said Evie, "Lydia could probably use a little help."

"Come any time, Evie, and tell Earl to come too."

"I have been canning apples all week. I will bring some apples for pies.

Laura peeled vegetables, and Martha helped wash pans, and carried water from the spring. Jane sat with John on her lap and asked him if he was happy in the new house. He bubbled and drooled and patted her cheek until she laughed.

"I am going to miss the boys real bad," she said to Lydia. "Please come home at Thanksgiving so we can see them again. We can only stay two or three days. We have to stop overnight at the inn in Petros, because we can't make it in one day. The boys will be expecting us back, and we don't want to worry them."

There were some good dinners prepared on the little stove, and Jane said she was proud of Lydia for making do like that. William took Jane around the property and she loved every bit of it. Will can fertilize and have some good crops here. He does need some help though. Don't tell him, but I am going to see if there is anyone around home that needs work. Will can afford to pay a man or two now, and get this place going."

When William and Jane prepared to leave, it was a sad time. The little boys were crying and reaching to their grandmother in the wagon, and Jane started to cry also. Dent and Martha waved as long as they could see the wagon in the distance.

Will said, "I have work to do." and he left for the barn." Lydia rocked John and George and comforted them. Then she said, "I have work to do too, George, you must be good so John won't cry." Martha came over and took both boys outside to play.

Kathleen Lawson lay in her bed listening to her mother and father arguing. It was about money. It was always about money. She had four sisters. She was the eldest. Stella was two years younger and the other three were under school age, Melinda, Dora and Hallie. Kathleen had always been her mother's helper. She had worked as far back as she could remember. Kathleen was eighteen now and she was sick of listening to her parents, Flora and Sam Lawson, fretting about making ends meet. As she lay there she developed a plan in her mind. She would get away. She would ask at church on Sunday if there was anyone who needed some work done in their house. If she could just get room and board, she would be satisfied. That way there would be one less mouth to feed. She may even be able to help her mother in some way. Satisfied with her decision, she said a prayer. "Please let me find a good family, so I can make a new start. Amen."

Dent went out to do chores and told his mother he wanted to go fishing, so they could have a change in their dinners.

"Sounds good, but go ask your father first."

Lydia said, "There is so much to do. She scrubbed clothes on a washboard, and hung them on a line in the yard. It was a very busy time. She dropped a towel on the ground, and Toby grabbed it and ran. As she chased him, she saw Will coming into the yard. and he was laughing.

"If you think it is funny to scrub dirt out on a washboard, then you should try it!" she yelled at him.

Will said, "Sorry," and went to help pull the clothes from the clothesline. Martha got the children inside.

Will said to Lydia. "I want to talk to you about something, Lydia. Sit down, the clothes can wait. There is a girl that Evie and Earl told me about that is 18 years old and lives with her parents and four sisters. She has been asking around church for work. Just a small wage, room and board, to get out of the house, and we can use her. What do you say?"

"I say it is a great idea. Does she live very far away?"

"I will go see Luther at the store and find out. What do you need from the store?"

A shower came up and Lydia worried about Dent at the creek. She needn't have been concerned, for he came into the yard with a huge string of fish. "I don't mind the rain," he said. "Sometimes they bite better when it rains." He got a pan and went to the side of the barn, and started to dress the fish.

Lydia said, "I will make corn pones to eat with the fish."

Martha had learned to knit. Lydia was a good teacher. They had made winter things and pieced quilt tops and prepared for the winter months. Martha showed her the sweater she was making and wanted her help. "After supper, Martha. We are having fish, and I need to make some bread. Sit down. Did you know we are going to have some help in the house? Will has gone to see about it now."

Dent came to bring the fish to his mother. Will's wagon was turning into the lane and there was someone with him. He rushed inside and told Lydia that company was coming.

Lydia hurried to the window and saw the girl. "I know her. She goes to church."

Will brought Kathleen inside with her suitcase. Will said, "Lydia, this is Kathleen Lawson. She has come to help us."

"Please call me Kathy," she said, "it is so much easier to say and I am used to it."

Martha said, "Mama, can Kathy share my room?"

"I think so, if she would like."

"I would," said Kathy. "It would help me not to miss my little sister."

Will had ordered another bed from Harness' Store, and it was due any day. "You will have to share a bed until the new one arrives," he said.

The next days were pleasant. Lydia and Kathy got on well. John and George loved Kathy, and she was a very good cook. Lydia felt better and did her work happily.

Martha said, "I learned to knit, Kathy, would you like to learn, too? Mama could teach you if you want to learn."

"We will ask her about it," said Kathy. "I'll see if she has time."

Will had taken one of the horses to the edge of the forest and chopped down four large oaks. He made a sled and the horse pulled the logs one at a time up to the place he had planned to build the barn. That night he was very sore and tired and went to bed early.

The next morning he told Lydia, "I am going into Harness' Store and buy a cook stove. I don't know when we will get that stove from Roane, and we need one."

"Good," said Lydia. "I'm glad."

"I'll get some more flour and baking powders, and we can have some biscuits for a change."

He returned with the stove and stovepipes in the wagon. Dent helped him as much as he could, and Lydia shoved a little, too. Finally it was up and Will tried it out.

"It works just fine," he announced.

Soon Lydia had biscuits started, and found that she really liked this new stove a lot.


Will rose early the next morning and had planned to go and trim the oak logs for posts for his barn. He milked the cow and fed the stock. He returned to eat, and Kathy had made biscuits and gravy with pork sausage. "It looks very good," he told her. Lydia set George up on the bench to eat and was feeding John. There was a shout from outside and Toby was barking. Will went out to the front porch. He saw in the lane a large wagon pulled by two beautiful black stallions. Two young men got down and approached Will.

"Hello, Mr. Wilson. I am Kirby Lee and this is Paul Redmond. Your father told us you might see your way to take on some help."

They climbed down and shook hands with Will, and nodded to Lydia who had come to the doorway.

"Come in, and welcome," said Will. "We'll talk about it".

Lydia asked if they had eaten and they replied that they had camped on the road and had started out before dawn and indeed were hungry.

Kathy said, "I will just fry more eggs and make some more coffee."

"Mrs. Wilson, Your mother-in-law sent you some things. She said she hoped you could use them all."

Dent said he would be glad to help unload the wagon after they had eaten.

Kirby told them he and his friend had signed up for some property in Roane county and needed money, and would be glad of a chance to work for Will.

"How are my folks?" asked Will.

"Just fine, Sir. They enjoyed their trip, and told me to tell you so."

When they had finished, Will and Dent helped put the barrels and baskets on the porch, and Kirby took the horses and wagon out to the enclosure where he turned them in with Will's horses. "Just leave the wagon there," said Will. "I haven't put up my barn yet, nor a place for the wagons."

Will told them about starting to build the barn, and that Earl and some others had told him to let them know when they had built the wall and were ready to raise the barn.

"You just tell us what to do and we will help."

They sat under a tree and discussed wages and when all three made a bargain and were satisfied, Will said, "Let's go back and let you fellows rest for a bit. That was a long trip."

*Chapter*

# NINE

Weeks flew by. With help, Will had made progress with his fields, and the barn was almost ready for the raising. Will told Earl at church that they could come if the weather was fair on Monday. A big meal was planned by the wives, and the men arrived ready to work early Monday morning. Dent helped to place make-shift tables in the yard, and Lydia spread tablecloths over them. Evie, Maggie, and the others placed their food there, and helped Lydia fry chicken and make biscuits and pies in the big range in the kitchen. It was a fabulous day, warm but pleasant, and the children were enjoying their visiting neighbor children at play.

The feast was ready and the men came and sat around devouring the delicious home cooked meal.

Will told them to let him and Lydia know when another barn would be raised so he could return the favor. "We want to help someone else as you have helped us!"

"I hear you are going to add on to your house, too," said Earl.

"Yes, after the garden is laid by, and the corn and wheat are growing well. I need another two rooms and a loft, and I want to extend the cellar, too."

Evie said, "Well, you have some good help here in Kirby and Paul."

She grinned at the two men enjoying the pieces of chicken and hot biscuits.

Elmer Creech told Will that he didn't recognize his old place, and it was looking real good. "We certainly have been busy, both Lydia and I, and also the kids."

They returned to work and afterward, Mr. Deems got his fiddle from his wagon and they danced to the music he provided. Before the shadows crept onward, Maggie said, "I think we better head home," Evie and Earl said, "We have to go, too. There is no one at home to feed the stock."

The Wilsons waved goodbye to their friends and cleaned up the yards. Kathy washed dishes and Martha helped to put them away, and Will lit the lamps. Lydia had already put the little boys to bed and said, "Will, I think I will turn in. I am tired tonight."

Kirby and Paul sat outside for a while. Kathy peeked out the window. She said to Martha, "I think that Paul is very handsome, don't you?" But Martha was already asleep.

The new bed had arrived, and now Kathy had her own. Lydia put a pretty quilt on it, and it looked very cheerful. The new quilts and homespun sheets that Jane had sent by Kirby were very welcome. Kathy brought some embroidered pillow cases from her home when she had visited there last Sunday. She had taken them from her hope chest.

Martha asked her, "What is a hope chest?"

"It is a box or chest that holds things a girl makes or buys to use in her own home later when she marries," Kathy explained.

There were other gifts in the barrels sent by Jane. Two beautiful vases were wrapped in the quilts and towels. Lydia recognized them. Lydia was so moved, she shed a tear. "I will get Earl to make me a table for the parlor this winter, and I will set these on it."

Martha was growing strong and browned as she worked with Dent and her father in the vegetable garden. William had sent a red rooster and three hens to Will and the flock was increased. Paul stretched more wire to the chicken lot, and added to the roosting area. There was an increase in eggs and plenty to trade in at the store for sugar and lard. Kathy was told to bake a cake and some bread to take home with her on her weekend visit. One rainy day after the boys were down for their nap, Lydia told Kathy she would give her a lesson in knitting. She showed her the stockings, mittens, and scarves she had a made for everyone to use when winter arrived. Martha was doing better knitting on her sweater too. Kathy learned quickly, and soon was making a muffler in a pretty reddish color. "I can make all my Christmas presents this way," said Kathy.

Lydia felt ill one day after cooking in the hot kitchen all morning.

"I think I will lie down a few minutes," she told Kathy. "Martha, help serve the dinner." When Will and the men came in, Will went directly to the bedroom to see Lydia.

"It's nothing, Will," she assured him. She had a wet washcloth on her forehead, and was lying in the big bed. "I'll be all right in a little while."

"I worry about you," said Will. "I guess it's the heat. You work too hard."

"Kathy has been a big help to me, Will. I don't do as much while she's here."

"I know," answered Will. "She sure knows her way around a kitchen! Her biscuits are almost as light as yours!" He laughed and kissed her. "After I eat, I am going back to the field. You stay in bed."

Kathy sent Dent to the woods to get some cherry bark "I'm going to make a tea for your mother."

He took his gun along in case he saw a squirrel. Paul and Kirby had taught him to shoot and hunt. He hooked the basket on his arm, and called out to his father that he was going to the woods for Kathy. It was a rule he always obeyed.

The woods were cool and shady. He walked under the spreading branches. A rabbit scurried behind a tree. Dent sat down on a log and waited as quietly as he could. There were probably more in the woods close by. Just then he saw a squirrel dart up a tree. He aimed and the small animal fell to the forest floor. Out ran the rabbit and darted behind another tree. Dent gathered the cherry bark. He tied the animals together and headed for home. He was quite proud of himself. Kathy was delighted with the game, and told Dent to hurry and skin them and dress them for the skillet. She made the tea and strained it and set it to cool. Martha peeled potatoes and got some new onions from the garden. Soon there were good smells coming from the kitchen. Kathy made a pan of cream gravy, and baked a pan of bread. Leaving Martha to oversee the cooking, she took a cup of tea to Lydia. She was propped up on pillows and said she felt a little better. Lydia took the cup.

"How smart of you, Kathy," she said. Kathy noticed that Lydia's face was pale, and she urged her to lie back after she sipped the tea.

"Did your mother teach you about herbs?"

"Yes, and so did my grandmother. I will teach you to make some different kinds if you like." Lydia lay back. "I'll bring you some supper after a while. You will never guess what I'm fixing!"

At the table, Dent told his father and the others about the grapes and cherries he saw in the woods. "There are lots of blackberry briers there, too. They are covered with green berries."

"We will have plenty to can and preserve for the winter," said Will. "Good work, Son."

The following day Lydia sat in her rocker feeling a little weak, but getting better, she told them. By supper time she was much stronger, and helped with John and George. Kathy set chores for Martha and Dent. Then she took a pan of new tender green beans to Lydia, who sat in her rocker on the porch. "If you will break these, I will go set some bread to rise."

Will and Kirby were talking as they returned to the house the following day. "Mr. Wilson, I wonder if Paul and I could take some of the lumber, and build a little cabin out past the alfalfa field. We could sleep out there and have more privacy. If Mrs. Wilson could spare it, we could put up the little heater out there and prepare our own breakfast. We will build makeshift beds, and a little table. Then this winter we can stay out there."

"If you really want to, it is okay with me. We will talk more about it later."

That night, Will asked Lydia if Maggie Creech wanted the little heater back. He explained the idea of Kirby and Paul wanting to build the little house.

"We can ask her. She said she was lending it to us."

"I think that is such a good idea," remarked Kathy. "It would be nice for them to have their own little place."

Will told Lydia, as he tore off the page of May from the calendar, "I want to think of some ways to add to our bank account."

"Are we in trouble?"

"No, Lydia. We have used a lot of our funds from Alabama, and there is no more of our farm to sell. I want to have money to add to the account for the children's school clothes and new shoes for all of us."

"Yes, and there will also be books to buy and slates and chalk for Martha and Dent."

Will said seriously, "I have been thinking that I can fell some of the oaks and chestnuts and haul them to the sawmill. They will pay top dollar for them."

"How will you get them there?" asked Lydia.

"We use chains and a special harness for the horses, and drag the logs to the mill. It is a long hard job, but it pays well, and we have the timber on our land already. The other trees will grow faster with more sunlight."

"I will try to think of something, too," said Lydia.

"You have enough to do with the house and children," he answered. "Now let's have some coffee."

When Lydia got up sick one morning, she suspected what was wrong. Then the next day in the outhouse, she was ill again. She was pretty sure then. "Another baby," she thought. "How can I tell Will? He is just talking about making more money for expenses. How can he be happy about another baby coming?" She decided to hold the news for a while. One morning after appearing pale, to the breakfast table, Kathy asked her about the new baby.

"How did you know?"

"My mother has had so many, I know the signs."she said and laughed.

"Let this be our secret. I haven't told Will yet."

Will used three horses in turn to drag the fallen logs to the mill He stopped just long enough to eat a quick dinner and then back to work. Dent took the horses back to the barn as Will changed the harness to the next one. Then he rubbed each horse down and fed them. Paul and Kirby helped pull the logs from the woods and piled them up. They, too, came in to eat and rest a few minutes and then went back. By sundown a weary and sore Will had a roll of bills and a smile to show Lydia, "Those boys need a day off. They have worked hard."

Lydia sat in her rocker and sewed up a rip in a pillow case. She was staring at the embroidery that adorned it when she had an idea. She called Kathy. "Look at this," she said.

"It is very pretty, "said Kathy, who had washed the case many times and knew the colors well.

"No, I mean, do you think you can do this embroidery?"

"I can do some of those stitches."

"I can teach you the others. I think I know how to get some money coming in to help with the children's clothes and shoes."

"I have to go. The bread is ready."

Lydia went inside her bedroom and got the writing paper. She started making a list. When she was called to the dinner table she gleamed with her secret. Will and the others came in for dinner and sat down.

"Will," asked Lydia. "Can you spare Kirby or Paul to take me over to see Maggie tomorrow? I haven't seen her in a while."

"Not since Sunday at church," said Will.

"I mean to talk to and visit," said Lydia.

"Let's see. I guess Paul can take you. I can order some meal, and he can go by the mill while you visit with Maggie."

The next morning, Lydia had the boys dressed and ready to leave when Paul brought the wagon around. She set a basket of eggs and another basket in the wagon. They were soon rolling down the road. George was chattering and very happy to be going out with his mother. Paul dropped them at Maggie's and said, "I will be back sometime after dinner."

Maggie was elated to see Lydia and the children. Lydia sent them to the back yard to play where Lenora could see them from her kitchen window. "I have some news for you. I haven't told Will yet. I am pregnant."

"How wonderful, Lydia." She got up and hugged her.

"Now, I have something to show you. Look at these scarves." She brought out her basket and handed her some scarves and a pillow case.

"They are beautiful. Did you do this embroidery and lace?"

"Yes. Now I was wondering if these would sell in Luther's store. I want to add to our money and this is one way I can do it."

"I really think they would. I would like to buy some for Christmas presents, if you are going to sell them."

"I haven't gotten that far yet," answered Lydia. "I wanted to talk to you and get your opinion."

Lenora brought the boys back and asked Lydia if they could have some apple juice and gingerbread. "Yes, if I can have some too!" said Lydia.

Then Lydia told Maggie that she meant to stop by the store and talk to Luther about it.

After a large dinner and a walk in the orchard, Maggie saw the wagon coming. "There's Paul already. Where did the time go?"

"Tell Paul to go eat dinner, and we will get you some peach preserves from the cellar. George. Do you like preserves?"

"I think so," answered George.

Lydia laughed. "That boy will eat anything sweet."

On the way to their home Lydia asked Paul if he would stop at the store. I want to take these eggs in and talk to Luther. Will you watch the boys a few minutes?"

She picked up the two baskets and went into the store. In a few minutes she returned with the mail and a sack of sugar and flour. "Now let's go home," she said.

When Lydia arrived home, John and George were put on their beds to nap. Lydia put her purchases in the pantry, and sat down in the kitchen to talk to Kathy.

"Sit down and have coffee with me, Kathy. I want to tell you that Maggie loved the pieces and Luther said he was sure he could sell some. He said he would keep the scarves, and show them to the tradesman when he came through, and would let me know. I told him it was a secret until I told him different."

"I am so happy for you. This is going to work. I just know it is." Kathy jumped up and said. "I don't want my cornbread to burn."

The first of July brought hot days and longer hours. The blackberries ripened and the grapes hung plentifully on the wild vines in the woods. Black walnuts were growing on the trees, and the white walnuts were not far behind. Dent and Martha picked berries and took Toby with them to warn them of snakes. They left early in the mornings and returned with loaded pails and happy faces. Lydia canned, made blackberry jelly and jam, and the shelves in the cellar were filling up quickly. Vegetables were ready to gather, and Will and Dent were busy, and Kirby kept long hours as he worked in the fields. Paul had suffered from severe sunburn and both Lydia and Kathy were treating him with burn remedies, and he was anxious to get back out to do his share of work.

Kathy told Lydia that she wanted to go picking berries with them at least one day. Lydia agreed. "You may go, Kathy, and remember you must take some of what you gather to your mother."

So the next morning, happily, Kathy set out with Dent and Martha with their pails and baskets. Lydia made the dinner and had it ready, fresh cabbage and new peas, lettuce and green onions from the garden. The men raved about the good dinner. When Kathy and Dent and Martha came in all tired and sweaty, they pounced on the plates to enjoy what Lydia had cooked. They had set their pails and baskets of blackberries on the back porch and washed up outside the door at the wash table.

Kathy said, "I will have to rest a bit before I can help with the canning."

Paul sat down beside Kathy with his face and arms smeared with the ointment which Lydia had applied for the sunburn. "I will clean up the dishes and wash canning jars. It is the least I can do. I want to get back out there as soon as I can, but this way, I can at least be busy."

Lydia said, "I appreciate that, Paul. You've got the job!"

Kathy lay down for a while and Martha sat on the porch breaking early beans. George was playing in the yard. Kirby had built a fence around the yard so the boys could not wander off. The gate was only a makeshift one, but he promised to make a good one when he had time.

When Kathy got up from her nap, Lydia was just getting the first batch of blackberries to boil on the wood stove.

"I'll get the jars sterilized," she told Lydia. "Thanks for letting me rest."

By supper time, there were several quarts of canned blackberries sitting on the work table. Lydia had warmed up the cabbage and had a pan of cornbread on the table with more fresh onions and a bowl of fried okra.

Will said, "I love fried okra."

"No kidding," said Lydia. "You have told us that many times."

She turned to Kathy. "Why don't you and Paul take the berries I left on the porch over to your mother, after the sun sets? That way Paul won't get more sun, and I think he will be much better by morning."

"I would love to," said Kathy. "I'll just change my dress after I get the dishes washed."

"Never mind," said Martha, "I will do the dishes."

So Kathy went to change and sat on the porch with Paul until the sun got low in the west. They loaded the berries and rode off. Will said, "That was nice of you, Lydia, Paul has been feeling really bad about missing work. Having some time with Kathy will put him in a good frame of mind."

Morning came and the rooster announced another working day. Kathy was making biscuits and Lydia was getting George and John dressed. There was a shout from outside and Dent went to see who was coming. Kathy said, "Oh my! It is Papa. She ran outside. Mr. Lawson called out. "We are going to another blackberry patch. Do you and Dent want to come with us? It is down by the Jamestown Road."

Dent asked his mother if he could go.

Lydia said, "Of course."

"This is the first time I have seen him interested in anything except his garden. I guess he liked the berries we took to Mama last night. Did you know that Papa has cleared more of his land and is putting in alfalfa and wheat?"

"I think that will be very beneficial later on."

"Yes. There will be some for sale, and it will bring in some extra money for all the school things and extra for Christmas."

Kathy was watching the children on the wagon.

"Would you like to go with them?"

"Oh, Yes. Thank you!" beamed Kathy. "Let me get my straw hat, and the pails and baskets from the porch."

Dent said, "I've already put everything in the wagon. Let's go!"

Lydia watched the enthusiastic bunch roll down the road. She turned to George, and said "How about a nice haircut today, young man?"

George ran and hid behind his father. "Let's go, boys, before she takes her scissors to us too!"

The next days were filled with picking tomatoes, beans, cabbage and okra. Everyone stayed busy. One day Evie came from town and had a basket full of apples. Lydia welcomed her with open arms. "I've come to show you how to make kraut," she said. "First, here are some apples for a pie for supper. You make better crust than I do, and Earl said to save him a piece."

Martha and Lydia got baskets and went to gather the cabbages, while Kathy washed the crock and Evie peeled apples for the pie. "I brought a couple of choppers. Don't let me forget to take them home. I need to make my own kraut in a few days. Earl loves kraut. We always make a lot every year."

All day they chopped cabbage and packed it down in the crock. "We'll add salt and cover it. Will can carry it down to the cellar, and every day you push it down into the brine and cover it back up."

When Lydia rang the gong for Will and the men to come for supper, they found a buggy outside the gate. Earl had come for supper and to take Evie home. Lydia said to Will, "He was afraid there would be no pie left after you saw it!"

Evie said, "That is why we made two pies!"

## Chapter

# TEN

When she had time, Lydia embroidered on her scarves. She had the new silk thread from Luther, with a note, saying the tradesman was interested in three dozen of the scarves, and they would get together on the prices. Lydia was very happy about this. She set Martha to helping Kathy in the kitchen, so she would have more time. She kept her work in a trunk in the back bedroom. When the beans came ready, she had to spend more time canning and making pickles from the cucumbers. Her days were very busy, but she remembered that she wanted to add to the bank account so she kept up her steady pace.

After one dozen was ready, she told Will that she wanted to go to see Maggie again. This time she wanted to go to see Dr. McDonald in town for an examination after she left Maggie's house. Will said he would let Dent drive her in because he was getting pretty good driving the team.

This time she left the little boys at home with orders to Martha to keep them out of trouble. Another basket of eggs was loaded into the wagon, and she carried her sewing basket. She only stayed at Maggie's a few minutes. Maggie paid her for the scarf she had ready, and Dent started off to the store. Mr. Harness was in the post office area when Lydia went in. She told Dent to stay with the wagon as she was in a hurry. Luther came out with her mail and called for his wife to come and get some stamps for Lydia. Then he took the basket of scarves and they agreed on a price for the tradesman. Lydia gave him the basket of eggs, and ordered more thread and this time some soft white material. Luther, I only had enough for one dozen. When the order arrives, send it out to me. One of the men will be coming in for mail or supplies."

She got some stick candy for the children and another dozen canning jars with lids, and joined Dent in the wagon. "Let's hurry home, Son, I am tired." She would have to wait to see Dr. McDonald, because Dent would wonder why she was stopping there. She would have to tell Will about the baby soon.

Dent and Kirby took the boys swimming one day. The weather had turned hot and it was after supper. He told Will the little boys would enjoy it and he would start to teach George to swim. Paul decided he would go, too, and got his fishing gear. "I will swim and then go farther upstream and fish a little."

"Fine," said Will, "Catch us a good one!"

Kathy had gone to the spring. She had not felt well that morning. She was concerned as she didn't usually have any problems. She sat down on the bank and thought to stay there for a few minutes. She thought, "Just a few minutes and I will be all right."

Lydia finished the soup and began to prepare the bread to rise. She wondered why Kathy was so long at the spring. She called Dent.

"Take this pail to the spring and get me some more water. See if Kathy is daydreaming out there."

Dent found Kathy slumped over on the ground next to the spring. He knelt and turned her over. She was very pale and her breathing was not steady. He rushed home in alarm and told Lydia.

75

"Go fetch your father and Paul," she said. She rushed to the spring and held Kathy.

Paul rode to get Dr. McDonald as fast as the horse could carry him.

Kathy was put to bed and Dr. McDonald came in his black buggy with Paul riding Jonas behind.

Kathy had stirred and asked what had happened. The doctor examined her and said she had a fever. He told Lydia what to do and sat by the bed for a long time.

I think she has a kidney infection. He gave Lydia some powders to dissolve in water to give to Kathy. "Keep water by her bed and see that she drinks it. I'll come back after I finish office hours this afternoon."

The entire household was stunned as Kathy lay in her bedroom unable to rise. Martha said, Mama, I will help with dinner and the boys. Whatever you want me to do."

Will told Paul to drive over to tell Mrs. Lawson to pack a bag and return with him. "She will want to be here with Kathy."

For days Kathy lay pale and tired, with her mother and Lydia doing all they could for her. The doctor came almost every day, giving her medicine and ordering broth and tea for her. Mrs. Lawson and her daughter, Stella, took turns sitting with Kathy, and the house was quiet. Everyone did their best to make things easier for Lydia and Martha to carry on with the care of Kathy and the house. Paul came in to see her at dinner time, and went back to work with Will in the fields.

A summer storm came up and Kirby, Will and Paul rushed home. Thunder sounded and lightning flashed ferociously over the house. Kathy was restless and turned in her bed. Paul came in and asked to sit with her. When they were alone he murmured to her and held her hand.

"You must get well, Kathy. I can't make it without you." He bowed over her hand and a tear slipped down. "Pray that God will make you well. We have been praying at church." Kathy weakly squeezed his hand, and he leaned over to kiss her. "You mean everything to me, Kathy." He stayed there until Mrs. Lawson said he must leave.

Ten days later, Dent came in to see Kathy.

"Martha and I start to school tomorrow. We miss you."

Kathy stirred, "Have I been sick that long?"

"It has been two weeks, Kathy. Are you better?"

"I do feel better, Dent. You must be good at school, and come and tell me all about it."

Mrs. Lawson said, "I'll go get you some bread and butter, and some tea. You need to get your strength back"

Lydia came in with a tray of soup and bread spread with marmalade. "I've brought you a nice snack. Try to eat it all."

During the next few days, Kathy got stronger and the doctor allowed her to sit up part of the day. Paul was elated and had high hopes that she would recover. He brought flowers into the room, and Kathy loved them. "I have been a terrible burden to everyone," she said.

Lydia said, "No more of that kind of talk. We all love you. You must get well and make us some more blackberry cobbler." Everyone laughed and left the room so she could nap.

Mrs. Lawson went home to care for her family, and Stella stayed to help Lydia. Kathy improved and sat on the porch part of the warm days. Dent and Martha came to tell her what had happened at school. George and John kept her company, as they watched Toby rush around the yard. Soon she was feeling much better, but Lydia wanted her to be very strong before she went back to her chores.

Maggie came over one day. She had Frank to bring her. Frank helped her down from the buggy seat, she went through the gate. "I'll bring your things," said Frank. Lydia rushed out to meet her. What a surprise, Maggie!" Maggie shut the gate and stepped up on the porch, "I just had to come and see how the kraut was doing."

"It's so good to have you. Frank, come in, won't you?"

"No, I need to go to the mill. I will be by later for Maggie."

Lydia welcomed Maggie into the parlor. "Sit down, Maggie. How have you been?"

"Can't complain," said Maggie. "I brought you some lace and white material. It was just in my bureau drawer. You need it, so I brought it over to you." She spread it out on Lydia's lap.

"Oh. It is beautiful," exclaimed Lydia. "I love it. You must take something for it."

"No," said Maggie, "Just give me some good blackberry cobbler and we will be even," and they both laughed. "I will sell some of the things when you get them finished for Christmas presents."

"Let's go see what Kathy is cooking for dinner." And they went to the kitchen.

*Chapter*

# ELEVEN

Will went to the store one day; there was mail from his father and from Alabama. Luther said, "Here is a package for Lydia. I'll put it in with your supplies. Here is some candy for the children. No charge."

Lydia dried her hands and took the mail. Will said, "There is a package for you, too. I wonder what it is."

"I think I know, Will. Come and sit down. I want to talk to you."

She set the box on the table and they went into the parlor.

"This sounds serious," said Will.

"It is," she answered. "You see, I wanted to make some money too. I started making dresser scarves to sell to Luther. The tradesman has taken some to sell on his route. I ordered more material, and that is what's in the package."

Will stared at her a minute. "I wanted it to be a surprise," said Lydia.

"It is for sure," said Will.

"I used the eggs for money to buy the thread I used. So now the money has started coming in, and I won't be using the egg money for that anymore."

"You never cease to amaze me, Lydia."

"I have another surprise. I am expecting another baby."

"Oh, Lydia," exclaimed Will. He jumped up and hugged her.

"You aren't disappointed?" asked Lydia.

"I am overjoyed, Lyddie. It is very good news."

"I thought it was maybe a bad time with school starting and everything."

"There is no bad time to have another child. We will plan for it."

Lydia said, "Let's go tell the rest of the family."

"I think we better wait until they come in to eat," said Will.

He and Paul had worked steadily and deserved the day off. At dinner, Paul said he would be happy to go by Mr. Lawson's house for Kathy that evening. "I have already told Kathy to wait for you," answered Will.

As they sat on the porch cooling off, Lydia said, "I thought Kirby had a girl back in Roane County."

"He does. What makes you think he has gone to see a girl?"

"We ladies must stick together," said Lydia. "I think I will lie down for a while."

When Lydia and Martha were cleaning up the supper dishes, Kirby came in. He had stabled his horse. "Anything left?" he asked.

"Of course! I'll get you a plate."

Afterward, he joined Will on the porch. "Will, do you remember we talked of raising bees?"

"Yes."

"I went to see Mr. Rutherford today. He lent me this book on raising bees." He handed Will a book. "Do you want to borrow it for a day or so?"

"That is a good idea. I did want to find out a few things."

"I thought we could work together and share the profits, if that is all right with you?"

"You've got a deal."

"Then, I think I will head out to the shack and change out of these clothes. Goodnight, Sir,"

"Kirby, don't call me 'Sir' any more. We are friends."

"Goodnight, Will," said Kirby, smiling.


In September, school started in Norma. Will registered Dent and Martha. They left on a warm morning, wearing new shoes and clothes and carrying new slates and chalk. They had been told their teacher would be Miss Twiddle and Dent laughed. "You better get all that out of your system and get off on the right foot with her," said Will. "She will give you both tests to see which grades to put you in before the lessons start.

They met others on the way, some from the church and some they didn't know.

They all approached the school in a merry frame of mind.

The school was a one room building. It had a pot-bellied stove next to one wall. On a bench near the door was a bench with a water pail sitting on it, and a dipper hanging on a peg above it. There were windows, and a huge blackboard.


That afternoon Will and Kirby went to the woods to gather black walnuts. They took two horses with sacks across the saddles and planned to get a good supply. Dent had told them, there were some white walnuts in the woods too.

"I'll string shuck beans, and onions to hang on the rafters in the cellar while you are gone," said Lydia. Paul had added more shelves for the canned fruit. The kraut was ready, and Lydia had made three kinds of pickles. They were very proud of all their hard work. The shelves held colorful fruits and vegetables.

The walnuts were put in a sunny place, behind the barn, to dry out so the hulls could be stripped off later. Kirby went to the trees, and gathered in all the fruit that was left so none would be wasted.

One morning, the pastor came to see Will. "May I talk to you in private?" he asked. They walked out toward the barn, and Pastor Green said, "Will, there some families that are going hungry. We are having a meeting at the church to see if we can gather some food between the members for these people. Some have had sickness and some are downright lazy, but we don't feel right letting their children suffer." "When is this meeting?" asked Will.

"It is this Sunday after church services. Will you and Lydia come?" When he discussed all this with Lydia, she said, "Will. I am not sure I should go because I am showing now, and some feel it isn't proper for ladies to go out in public this far along."

"It is up to you. If you don't feel comfortable, don't go. I will see what they decide and tell you about it."

On the following Monday, Pastor Green's wagon appeared at the gate. Lydia and Will had gathered some contributions of food for the cause. He felt that no family should go hungry. He said, "Pastor, when we go hunting again we will try to get some game for these folks, too."

"I'll go right now," said Dent.

Will laughed. "Get in there and study your books. We can go hunting another time."

On Saturday Martha was peeling potatoes in the kitchen helping Kathy. She was trying to hurry so she could go outside out of the heat of the stove. All at once the knife slipped and hit her left hand. She screamed as the blood poured over her dress. She was terrified. While Kathy went to ring the dinner gong to summon Will from the field, Lydia bound Martha's hand with a towel trying to staunch the flow of blood. Will saddled Jonas quickly and rode to the door of the cabin. He put Martha up in front of him, and told Kirby to bring Lydia in the buggy, and meet him at Dr. McDonald's office.

Dr. McDonald said, "This will need stitches. Martha, you must be very brave." He and his nurse took Martha to one of the back rooms.

After the stitches were placed, the doctor told Lydia to keep her quiet. He said, "Here are some papers of powders. Put one in a half cup of water and give to her every four hours for pain."

Martha rode in the buggy with Kirby and Lydia. At home she was pale and shaky. Lydia put her to bed at once and gave her one of the doses of medicine. Kathy was worried and asked Lydia when she went to the kitchen for a cup of coffee, if Martha was going to be all right.

Lydia explained everything, and Will arrived for a cup of coffee too. "What a scare," he said. "It could have been much worse." Martha had to have help changing clothes, and didn't go to school for the rest of the week. When Miss Tweedle sent her work to do on her slate, Dent carried it back the next morning. Kathy sat and talked to her when the days got boring, and the hand started healing. Kirby made her a sling, to support her hand, and took her out in the buggy to pick up the mail and run errands. This helped her morale. Lydia sat with her and told her stories of her grandmother back in Alabama and her great grandmother, too.

Will and Kirby cleared the small bean patch of its vines and sewed turnips there. The tops made tasty greens cooked with a ham bone. Paul found a bee tree, and he and the others took a horse and cart into the woods to take the honey from it. They lit a smudge fire and let the smoke drift up and calm the bees, then chopped the tree down and took the honey and comb from the tree. It was delicious and they had plenty share with the Creeches and Earl and Evie. Dent went fishing in one of the streams farther up on Will's land, and caught three large buffalo fish, native to the area. They were huge fish some weighing as much as two or more pounds each. He sent some to Pastor Green to share with some of the families who were hungry.

Martha was getting better, and looking forward to getting back to school. She had kept up with all her lessons.

Lydia had Paul to take her and Martha into Harness' store one day, where Luther and his wife fussed over Martha and gave her peppermint sticks. There was a package from Roane County which Paul took to the buggy. Luther showed Lydia the book with their records, and paid her what was due her for the fancy needlework that had been sold. It was quite an improvement over the last time. Lydia was very pleased, and Luther handed her the new order from the tradesman.

"I better order more thread." she said. "I don't have time to make this much lace, I will have to buy some." She left Luther a sample of her latest designs on a dresser scarf to show the tradesman.

"It is very pretty, Lydia. I know it will go over well."

*Chapter*

# TWELVE

Lydia was not feeling good and sat in her rocker. Her skirts had been let out and she wore huge aprons over her swelling body. Kathy was back doing all the work, with help from Martha when she was home from school and on the weekends. Lydia sewed and embroidered to catch up on the orders she had promised Luther. Kathy had also done several scarves and pillowcases for her hope chest. She told Lydia, "Why don't you take these of mine to finish your order for Mr. Harness?"

Lydia said, "I wouldn't want to do that, Kathy."

"Please, I feel bad that all of you tended me and I couldn't work. This will make me feel I have done something back. I can always make more."

"All right, if it will make you happy," said Lydia, "These will be the last of Mr. Harness' order for Mr. Fleming, the tradesman. I will get Will or Paul to take them in for me. He will probably have another order by now."

On October 12$^{th}$, the weather changed. Frost covered the ground, and more wood was gathered for winter fires. The woodpile grew and Will put a tarp over it to keep it dry.

Kirby went around the cabin chinking the cracks that let drafts in, and Paul chopped wood for their little hut on the hill. Kathy went to the little cabin, and cleaned and put a cloth on the table that Kirby had made and put a braided rag rug on the floor. Lydia sent new quilts so their bed would be warmer. Kathy was glad to be doing these things for Paul and every time she thought of him her face glowed.

Lydia told Kirby, "When the nights get too cold, you must come back to the house. I don't want you and Paul to be out there freezing."

At supper, Will asked Lydia, "Do we have enough lard cans and jars for sausage? It will be cold enough to kill hogs before long."

"If you are going to kill two, we will need to get more cans for the lard. I have plenty jars. I got some with my last profit."

"Kirby, we need to think about building the smokehouse."

"Yes," answered Kirby. "We need to go to the woods for some hickory to burn too."

"Saturday, Dent and I will go get the hickory, and you and Paul go mark some trees to cut for the smokehouse. I won't buy lumber for that. We have plenty timber to use, and we will trim the limbs for firewood."

"Looks like some busy days ahead," said Kathy.

The next morning at daybreak, Will and the others dressed warmly and went after breakfast to the forest. Lydia and Kathy tidied the house and put dinner on to cook. Martha made beds. Then she put the boys' coats on them and took them for a short time outside. The dead leaves were blowing in the wind and John lost his hat. Martha went chasing it, and stopped with her mouth dropping open when she saw a black carriage coming down the road. It turned into the lane, and Martha called out to her mother. "Come quick. It's Grandpa!"

Lydia looked out the window and saw her father and mother in the carriage. Lewis was driving the team and

James was sitting beside him. In the seat behind was Anna George.

Lydia rushed out to welcome them and hugged her parents and brother. "What a surprise! You should have written."

"We wanted to surprise you. Where's Will?"

"Come inside. Will and the others have gone to the woods to get hickory trees."

James carried the cases to the porch and went back to help his father carry a big crate to the house. Then the trunk was brought. Martha ran up to greet her grandparents. "My, how the boys have grown," said Anna. "And my little Martha is so tall and strong!"

Kathy stood in the doorway. "Meet Kathy Lawson. She's my right arm," said Lydia.

"Kathy, this is Lewis and Anna George, my parents, and this fine fellow is my brother, James. Let's go inside. Is anyone hungry?"

Lewis said to Lydia, "This one is always hungry!"

Will and the others came in by dinnertime and learned of his guests. "Lewis, you couldn't have picked a better time to come. We are killing hogs in a day or two."

James said, "Just my luck!"

Everyone wanted to catch up on the news. Martha was wondering what was in the crate. Kathy poured coffee. When everyone had eaten all they could hold, Kathy said, "Have more coffee, Mr. George."

"Please, call me Lewis. And this is Anna."

"I'll try to remember."

"How did you get here?" asked Will.

"We rode the stagecoach to Jacksboro, and rented the carriage. We hired it for a week."

Will told them how proud he was of Paul and Kirby. They seem like my own family."

"Let's go out on the porch," said Anna, "I want Lewis to open the crate and show Lydia her present."

"Bring a crowbar, Will," said Lewis. James opened the crate and brought out a beautifully carved cradle. "This is for our new grandchild."

Lydia exclaimed, "It is beautiful!"

"Martha, I have other things that we will get to later, so don't feel left out."

"Lewis, are you too tired to ride over the farm and see what we've done?"

"I think I can manage it," laughed Lewis. "I think these two want to chat anyway."

They woke up Sunday morning when the rooster crowed. Anna got up first, and told Lewis she wanted to go to church with the family. Lewis said, "If you don't mind, I'll stay here and rest up a bit."

"Kathy said she would stay, and start the dinner and not go to her mother's today. Kirby said, "I will stay here too. I want to read up on the bee business." After they left, Lewis and Kirby walked out to the barn and they discussed where the bee hives would be placed, and Kirby showed Lewis where he and Paul slept. We will be moving back to the house after the first snow. We may set the laundry heater up in one of the back bedrooms so the children will be warmer."

"Sounds good to me," said Lewis. "Now, where will this smokehouse go?"

Kathy had made a huge dinner, and it was a merry crowd that gathered around to eat. Anna said, "This girl can really cook. I may steal her away from you." Kathy smiled.

"We couldn't manage without Kathy."

On Monday, Evie and Earl came to help with the work. Will, Kirby and Paul went to the woods to fell the trees, and Dent and Martha went to school. James trimmed the branches off the hickory that Will had cut and brought home on Saturday.

While the smoke house was being raised, Kathy and Lydia showed Anna some of the fine embroidery and pillow cases she was preparing for the next order. Anna admired it and told Lydia she was proud of her. "I can send you lots of material. I don't do that kind of work anymore. I have some things in one of the cases for the baby. Jan and Mary sent things, too. They said to tell you they are very happy for you." She unpacked some little shirts and baby gowns, tucked and lacy, and some flannel night gowns. You can't have enough baby clothes, Lydia."

The place became a beehive of activity, as the smoke house was raised and the roof put on. There were open spots around the eaves for smoke to rise and the shelves were put in for the meat. Hooks were placed to support the hams and shoulders, and there was no wooden floor because the fires must be built to smoke and cure the meat. Clouds moved over along with a cold wind. Lewis shivered.

"Will, you should kill the hogs while we are here to help you. I want some good fresh pork anyway."

"We got the smokehouse up just in time," said Will." I think it is cold enough. We may as well start in the morning, Lewis. Are you up to it?"

"I am fine," said Lewis. "I'll drag out my sweater to put under my coat."

Earl said, "I will bring the lard cans out from the store as I come tomorrow. I will put them on your account. Is there anything else you need?"

Lydia said, "We need boxes of sage and black pepper."

Will said, "And pick up the mail for us, if you don't mind. We will get an early start here."

Everyone was ready for a good night's rest. Before it seemed time, the roosters were crowing and Will rose and called to Dent and Martha to get up. "You can help feed before you go to school."

Kathy started the breakfast, as Lydia came in and put her apron on. "I wasn't sure I wanted to get up this morning. When I remembered that good smell of pork frying, I came awake fast."

The big stove was fired up, soon the biscuits were browning in the oven and the gravy was bubbling in the pan. Anna came in help set the table.

Will stepped out of the house. He built a fire under the big iron pot in the back yard and filled it with water. Evie and Earl came with all the supplies and the mail. Evie put on a huge apron. Will went back inside to eat.

"Have some breakfast, you two," he said to Evie and Earl.

"We've eaten, but we can have some coffee and a biscuit with honey before we start to work."

Anna said to Lydia, "I will look after John and George for a while."

The new smokehouse stood ready and Toby was beside himself with all the activity. Will called for Paul to put him in the fenced yard so he would not be underfoot. Evie peeled potatoes and started a stew, and Lydia went to the spring house for butter and milk. Kathy gathered eggs and set bread to rise, and helped Lydia start the soup. "We better make cornbread enough for two or three meals," Lydia said. "We will be too busy frying meat and dressing out the pork and liver, to do it later."

All the men went out to work. It was a busy day for everyone. James, Kirby and Paul cut up the meat. Will and Lewis had done the killing and scraping while the hogs hung, headless from supports on the side of the barn. A long make-shift table sat in the back yard where Kirby worked. Another was used for salting and pans were set for pieces of liver and loin to be taken inside and fried for supper. Will came in for a brief rest, and Lewis said he had had enough, and went to lie dawn. Kirby and Paul came in for a snack and coffee, and then went back to take the salted side meat to the shelves in the smokehouse. Will cut up the liver and put it in pans. Kirby brought him the hams which he hung on the hooks, and Paul carried the shoulders to the smokehouse. Earl cleaned up, and helped dispose of the waste and Will helped to take down the tables and stack them against the barn.

He said to Earl, "I will get them cleaned tomorrow. We need to quit and go eat supper. You and Evie pick out what you want, and we will get it loaded for after you eat supper."

The aroma of pork frying and hot biscuits laced inside with honey, tempted them all to come and eat. Lydia poured up a huge bowl of cream gravy, while Kathy put another skillet on the stove to make another bowlful. With so many to eat, one was not enough.

"This is so good," said Anna. "I've never tasted better."

Martha took John and George out to a back room and gave them a quick bath, for they had dripped grease and gravy all over themselves. "Clean nightshirts for you two and here are your night caps. The night is too cold to sleep without them." She kissed them and put them to bed.

Kathy and Anna cleaned up the kitchen while Lydia sat by the fireside. "It has been a long day," she said. "I think I will have an early night."

Kathy said, "I'll take care of the food, Lydia. Just rest easy, and go to bed. The boys are already asleep."

Evie and Earl said goodnight and departed, tired but happy.

Kirby and Paul went toward their hut with the promise to come back at daybreak. That is when Will and Lydia and Kathy planned to cut up fat meat and make lard. Kathy and Martha retired to their rooms. Getting into their flannel gowns, they went over the long day. "We don't want to have many days like this one! We have enough pork to last up into the spring, I think."

"Mama will want you to take some home to your mother," said Martha.

They climbed into bed. "Mother and Papa are going to kill hogs this week too. But we will take some, so they can have a few good meals before that."

"Did you know that Kirby and Paul like the pork brains with eggs?" asked Martha.

"Ugh." said Kathy.

"They took some along with them. And bread and eggs too. Paul is going to fry them up for breakfast!"

"What a thought to go to sleep on. Goodnight."

Lydia tried to keep calm as the fat meat was cut up in chunks for the rendering. Finally she gave up and retired to the parlor to embroider on a new scarf. Anna said. "Sometimes expecting makes one queasy like that when they smell the meat, especially early like this. She needs a good sit-down anyway."

Outside Will and Kirby built up a hot fire under the pot. He poured in a cup of grease to get it started then James poured in a pan full of the meat. Kathy, Paul and Dent were busy cutting up more for the pot, while Martha washed and dried the cans. They sat waiting to receive the lard.

Anna dried the dishes and put them away and then joined Lydia and George and little John in the parlor. Anna said, "You are happy here aren't you, Lydia?"

"Yes, we have been doing pretty good here, and I have grown to love the mountains and the people."

Anna said, "You know that Rafe and one of his sons were killed in a barroom fight. I can't say I am sorry."

"Mama, that is all in the past. Let's just forget about it."

"But he took my family away from me that night," said Anna. "I can't forget that."

"We are happy here, Mama. Will has made a home for us, and he has enjoyed being back where he was raised."

"All right, we will say no more about it." She picked up a little wagon that George had just thrown down. "Where did this come from?"

"Kirby carves things when he is resting sometimes. He is teaching Dent to carve now, too. There is plenty of wood available, so there is no overhead. He plans to get some of his work to market this winter. He is going back to see his folks for Thanksgiving."

"Yes, I heard Kathy talking about it. She says Paul is going, too."

# THIRTEEN

Maggie sent word that Lydia and Anna were invited to a quilting bee at her home the next day. Kathy asked Lydia if she felt up to going.

Anna said she would like to meet all of Lydia's friends. So it was agreed that when Martha and Dent got home from school to look after John and George, she and Kathy and Anna would attend the party. Kathy said, "I will make a pie to take. Which kind should I make, Lydia?"

Lydia said, "Apple, and make one for here. We will have enough cooked for supper, and the men can serve themselves."

Kirby took them over to Maggie's house where the party was already started. Several ladies were quilting around the frames set up in Maggie's dining room. "I guess we will all eat in the kitchen," she told them.

Everyone had brought dishes of food. Lenora had made beef stew, and had coffee and tea for them to drink. Anna was introduced, and Kathy went to help Lenora in the kitchen.

"This is so much fun," she said. "It isn't even like work. Lydia needed to get out for a while, too." They chatted while Lydia, Maggie and the other guests sat around the frames.

Anna said, "I haven't quilted in so long, but I still remember how."

Will came for them about dark, and soon Lydia was ready to get into her nightgown and go to bed. She was very glad to get home.

The next morning, Will and the others gathered in the yard. A huge fire was built under the iron pot. Chunks of fat meat and pork skins were dropped into the steaming grease. The cans were ready to receive the hot lard.

Lydia was feeling more rested. While Kathy helped out side, Lydia and Anna cut up meat for pork sausage.

"When it is ready, we will grind it and put in the pepper and sage."

Outside Kirby and Paul poured up the lard and more meat was put into the steaming kettle. It was hard work, and the smoke blew back on them several times.

"I suggest we take off for a few minutes," said Will, "and go in and visit with the ladies awhile."

Paul said, "Go ahead, I will stay and feed the fire and stir the pot. I'm not tired."

It was a busy time inside as the sausage was put through the grinder and cooked on the stove. It was then put into hot half gallon glass jars, and turned upside down on the work table. Anna told Lewis when he came in to rest, "We will bring some tea into the parlor and join you. Then you can lie down for a while, if you like."

Will agreed. "You didn't come up here to work."

Lewis said, "I have enjoyed every minute since I have been here. Maybe we can take one day to go hunting though. I really want to do that before we leave."

"We sure will," answered Kirby and Will together. "We love to hunt. It isn't work!"

When Dent and Martha returned from school, Dent said he wanted to be included in the hunt. "Remember your promise to the pastor, Papa."

"I remember."

"I'll go out and help Paul," said Kathy. When the door closed behind her, Anna asked Lydia if they were courting.

"Yes, they are sweet on each other," said Lydia. "He has been taking her to her mother's house on the weekends, on the times she wants to go home, and going after her on Sunday nights."

They all rested the next day and chatted. Lewis went in the evening to be with Dent and Will when they fed the stock and milked the cow.

Lewis said to Will, "You should get a bull, Will."

"Maybe after Christmas," Will answered.

It was decided they would go hunting on Saturday since Dent was off from school. They got up early and took a wagon. They went into the mountains that belonged to the lumber company. Farmers were allowed to hunt there. Kirby, Paul and James climbed into the wagon, and Dent rode on one the wagon seats between his father and grandfather. He waved goodbye to Martha who had just gotten up and peeped out. Dent waved to her and they set off happily.

"Bring us back a buck," said Kathy, as she waved them off.

"We have the day to ourselves," said Lydia. "We must make the best of it!"

Anna agreed. "All I want to do is rock and visit with my grandsons and Martha. I need some memories to take back with me."

Martha jumped up and hugged her. "I love you, Grandma," she said.

"That is what I like to hear." Anna said.

Lydia said, "We should do some embroidery. I am getting way behind on my orders."

Kathy said, "I need to make some pillow cases for my hope chest." So all morning they talked and sewed and then fed the boys their lunch.

George said, "I want to go gather eggs."

"Me too," said John. Martha dressed them warmly and they went outside.

"Martha is growing up fast, isn't she?" asked Anna.

"Yes, she is, and I expect she will be a great help when the baby comes. I have a chest full of clothes for it. I may have to start sewing clothes for a two year old if this keeps up. I hope I don't have twins. They run in Will's family. Did you know that?"

"No, I didn't."

"Will is a twin himself. Jesse is his twin."

"You don't look like you are carrying twins," said her mother.

That evening before dark, Will returned and unloaded the wagon. Dent took it to the barn and rubbed the horses down and fed them.

Kirby was all smiles. "That big buck is mine," he said, "but you can all share it!" They also had a turkey, a wild boar, two quail, and a brace of rabbits.

"We need to share all this."

"Of course, I intend to. I will talk to Pastor Green tomorrow. He can come by and bring his wagon. Dent really did well. He shot the turkey and one of the rabbits."

"Good work, Dent," said his mother. "What about you, Paul?"

"Don't mention it," said Paul. "I only got one quail, and Kirby will not let me forget it!"

It was well past dark when all the wild game was skinned and cut up. The lanterns were lit, and a fire burned to keep them more comfortable. Every pan, pail, and tub available was put into use for all the meat.

"It was a good day, Lewis. I hope you got your fill of hunting," said Anna. "He will be bragging for weeks when we get home."

"And rightly so," said Lewis. "I want to tell my boys the old man can still shoot."

The next day Anna and Lewis went to church with Will. Lydia stayed home and prepared dinner. Kathy went home after church to see her family. Martha set the table and helped with the meal. They had venison for dinner and put the rabbit, quail and wild boar meat in the smokehouse where it froze solid. Pastor Green and his wife came to dinner and took back meat for the families that needed food and a venison steak for themselves.

In the afternoon, Lewis said, "It is getting colder. It snows here earlier than down home. We need to be leaving. We have hogs to butcher too, the boys and me."

Anna said, "I suppose so. Let me make the children some gingerbread this afternoon. I promised them, and if we are leaving, I better do it."

Lewis packed some of his clothes, and then shared the gingerbread with the children. After supper, Anna and Lydia packed her suitcases, and they spent their last moments before bed talking about the baby.

They rose early on Monday morning and packed the carriage. Martha said goodbye and went to do chores. Kathy said her goodbyes and returned to the house to make sure John was all right.

Lydia cried as she parted with her parents and wished them well, and invited them back whenever they felt like coming. "James, please bring them back. We loved having all of you."

James assured her he would try, and told her to be careful and not overdo.

"Will, take care of our girl," said Anna. "Let us know when the baby arrives, as soon as you can."

Lewis hugged Lydia and all the children. "Will," he said, "thank you for a very enjoyable visit. Come to see us when you can and bring the family." They stayed until the carriage was out of sight and sadly went inside.

*Chapter*

# FOURTEEN

On the last day of October there was snow on the ground when they woke. Since it had turned colder, Kirby and Paul had moved back to the house. After breakfast, Will and Kirby started to shovel snow. They made a path to the barn, outhouse, chicken run, and the smokehouse. When a path was cleared to the barn, Paul went to milk and take care of the stock, gather eggs and feed the chickens. They shivered and rushed back to warm themselves at the fireplace. They left their boots on the back porch. Dent and Martha stayed home from school and sat down with George and John to entertain them. The kitchen was well stocked with firewood, and the big stove glowed red as the stew was simmering, and the coffeepot was well used. Lydia churned and molded the butter, and Kathy poured up the buttermilk. It was cold enough to leave inside the house, but a path had to be shoveled to the spring for water.

Kirby told Dent it was a good time to teach him more about carving and asked if he would like to start a bird this time. Martha got her knitting out and sat with Lydia in the kitchen to finish the stockings she was making for her father.

"Mama, what do you think you will name the baby?"

"I don't know, honey. Do you have a name picked out if it is a girl?"

"I think I would like to her to be called Caroline."

"That is a pretty name. I think your father would agree to that."

When it snowed for three days, Dent and Martha started to fret, staying inside so much. Will said, "Come, boys and get your coats and mittens on. We are going to make a snowman."

Both screamed with delight and rushed for their coats and caps. "George and John can watch from the window. I don't want them to get an earache again," said Lydia.

After the snow thawed, the barnyard was a slush of mud. Will put some boards down at the worst places. He put ashes from the fireplace and stove on the path to the outhouse and the chicken run.

A man came to Will's house one day. It was a raw and windy day, and Will asked him in. He shook hands with Will and Kirby who was teaching Dent to carve an owl.

"My name is Hubert Gaines. I am in a bad strait of events, Sir. I am not here to ask for charity. I want to sell you a sow and two shoats." He named a price.

Will said, "Sit down, Mr. Gaines, and get warm. Dent, would you go tell your mother to bring some coffee?"

"I am sure we can do business. I have just killed two hogs, and we can start on another one. I am afraid we will have to go to town to the bank. When would you suggest we go for the sow?"

"I live on Brimstone," he said. Since the snow has melted, the road is very dangerous. It's better if I bring them down to you. I am more familiar with its twists and turns. How about tomorrow about two, and that will allow you time to get your cash from your bank." He rose to go. "I need to go to Harness' store and get some things. I can tell him now that I can pay up my bill tomorrow."

"Let us give you some venison to take home for your supper," Will rose to go outside with Mr. Gaines.

At that moment Lydia came in with a brown package and handed to the man. "I do appreciate this, Mr. Wilson."

By morning the ground was frozen and temperature had dropped. Will did his chores and ate a hearty breakfast. "I will be going in to the bank, Lydia, Do have anything you want delivered to the store?"

Martha said "Mama I need more yarn for the stockings. May I have more today?"

"Give your father a sample of the yarn you are using, and tell him how much you want. It will go on my account for the scarves, and Luther and I will settle when I go in again."

Kathy told Will, "Since you are doing that for Martha, will you get me some red silk thread? I will give you a piece to go by."

"Then hurry, both of you, before I change my mind," laughing as he said it. "Give me your list too, Lydia. What do you need from Luther's?"

Lydia laughed. "Just get us some sugar and a bottle of maple syrup. We have been using honey and we need a change."

That afternoon, Mr. Gaines arrived driving his mule that was more surefooted than a horse, pulling the wagon holding the sow and two pigs. Dent directed him up to the pigsty, went along behind the wagon. As they entered the house, Lydia had coffee ready and slices of apple pie. As he sat at their table with them, he told them he had two sons at home under five years old and had been working at the saw mill on Buffalo creek. Their canned things had run out and they needed some food. He could see his way through now until planting time again and he meant to raise more food if possible next summer. Will paid him for the hog and pigs and got a receipt. Then Mr. Gaines said he must go and do some business in town.

Will and Dent went up to feed and water the hog and see to the stock. "More good ham for next winter when we get these fattened up," he said.

Martha and Dent returned to school, glad to get out of the house. Kirby took them on one of his horses and returned in the afternoon.

Dent said to his father. "I was raised up another grade today, Papa; I am into the sixth grade books now."

"Wonderful,"

Lydia set Dent and George to cracking black walnuts and removing kernels for a cake. Everyone needs something different. The days were long and they were all accustomed to working hard, so the idle hours were wearing on the patience of some of them. Martha churned the sour milk for butter, while Lydia baked the cake. She sat in the edge of the parlor so the vibrations would not cause the cake to fall.

Martha said, "It smells so good. I want to learn to bake one."

Kirby and Paul came in from the barn. "Something smells mighty good in here."

Kathy said, "I expect I better learn this recipe, too."

During the first days of November, Dent and Martha told their parents there was to be a Thanksgiving play at school. Martha said she would be a Pilgrim and Dent would be an Indian. "It sounds like fun." said Lydia.

"All the parents are supposed to come," said Dent.

"We'll see," said Will.

The day before Thanksgiving, Kathy's bags were all packed. Paul had asked her to go with him and Kirby on the train to Roane County. He said he wanted her to meet his parents. Kirby was going to see his parents also. She helped Lydia bake the pumpkin pies, and then went to dress her hair the way she wanted to wear it tomorrow.

At dawn, Will took them to Bowling Station, where they bought passage on a coal car that was attached for passengers. The train was taking on water. When they boarded, Will told them to enjoy the trip and went inside to warm up before he started back.

Will stopped at Luther's store. He picked up a package for Lydia, the letters and some supplies and drove toward the Lawson home. Stella was already there on the little porch with her small trunk. Will spoke to Mrs. Lawson and then took up the trunk.

"We had best hurry, Stella, as it looks like snow again."

Will hurried down the rutted road toward Norma.

"Is your family planning to have a big Thanksgiving?" he asked Stella.

"Yes, Papa killed a turkey and mama is baking a pumpkin pie."

"We had so much turkey when my in-laws were here, that we decided to have chicken and dumplings," said Will.

They drove into the lane as big, fat snowflakes came down. Will carried her trunk in, and Lydia welcomed her warmly. "Tell Dent to fill the wood boxes, Lydia. It is snowing again."

"He already did that and fed the chickens and gathered eggs," said Lydia.

Will carried the trunk into the room Stella would share with Martha.

"You don't mind sharing," asked Lydia.

"No, I would love to share."

"I'll go take the buggy to the barn," said Will.

Stella settled right in, and started to help Lydia in the kitchen.

The next morning everyone was up early knowing it was a special day. Lydia started cooking the minute breakfast was over. Good food smells came from the kitchen, and the fires roared in the fireplace and cook stove. Everyone was toasty warm. Will sat and rocked his little ones and Martha knitted in the corner.

The meal was a great feast with chicken and dumplings, green beans, (canned the past summer) and Will declared he could not hold another bite. He took George and Dent to play in the snow, and after that said he was ready for pumpkin pie.

Will went to pick up Kirby, Paul, and Kathy at the station in New River where the coal train had added a passenger car. Kathy was fretting because the black soot had ruined her new cloak.

"But I am very glad to be back," she told Will.

At home she showed Lydia and Stella her present from Paul's mother.

"It has been in the family for years. She held out a gold locket and opened it to reveal a place for two pictures. "I asked Paul to have a picture made to go in the right side, and I'll put mine in the left."

That night Paul told them, "I have asked Kathy to marry me and she has said she would." There were hugs all around and Will congratulated both of them.

## Chapter FIFTEEN

Christmas was in the air. There was a church service where Pastor Green spoke to his congregation. The children put on a play for their parents. A tree stood in the corner, and after carols were sung, gifts were given. Everyone got a small bag of candy and nuts. Little George was wide-eyed at the special celebration. Will brought his family home and gave a treat to Lydia who had stayed home.

On Christmas morning, presents were given to the children and everyone watched them as they opened each one. Will had made a sled for each child, and Lydia had made a new shirt for each of the boys and dresses for the girls. Kirby gave out his gifts of carved animals and to Will a new hat. Lydia received new knitting needles and embroidery hoops. The others exchanged their gifts and Lydia went to the kitchen to start the dinner. Kathy had already baked two pies and gone home to be with her family.

Lydia stuffed a turkey with sage and chestnut dressing. She had glazed yams with honey, and cooked a pot of green beans that she had canned during the summer. Homemade bread with butter and a bowl of mashed potatoes were added. Then the pies and jam cake were served. Will and Kirby took their coffee to the living room and Paul said he wanted to go see the Lawson's before supper.

Dent said he was stuffed and wanted to go see about his traps and asked Will if he could take George with him.

"Yes, but you be extra careful and watch him every minute."

That afternoon, Will took Lydia to the barn to show her his Christmas present. It was in the loft. He brought it down and she was delighted to see he had bought her a spinning wheel. She had been learning to spin at Maggie's house. "It was her idea. Do you like it?"

She hugged Will and said, "Oh, I love it."

"Let's stay out here awhile before we go back." said Will.


January brought more snow and deep drifts. There were plenty of new recipes tried by Lydia and Kathy. The cabbages were dug up from their storage pit. Dent, Paul and Kirby went hunting often, and all the sleds came out that the boys and Martha had gotten for Christmas. Evie and Earl came over, and brought Maggie on his sled. Maggie admired the new spinning wheel. "Now you can practice spinning when you can't work outside."

Will had grown flax and had saved some of it for Lydia to spin into cloth. Maggie and Martha went into the kitchen and made molasses cookies. Kathy watched Lydia at the spinning wheel. "I want to learn that," she said.

That afternoon Dent called from outside. "Paul has killed a deer. Come and see." It took the men the rest of the day to butcher the buck. Paul was beside himself that he had actually brought down this huge animal. Kirby couldn't tease him anymore.

Maggie, Evie and Earl took some meat home with them after they had enjoyed venison for supper. Lydia had also wrapped some jam cake for them to eat later.

The next day Dent took the children to another spot on the farm to use their sleds. They had a wonderful time. Dent held John as he slid down the bank and he laughed with glee. George insisted he was big enough to go down by himself.

That night Lydia was up half the night with George for he had an earache. She put warmed sweet oil in his ear and sat rocking him for hours, vowing to herself that she would not allow him to go sledding any more.

The next day, Earl drove up with his sled. Paul said, "Will, I asked Earl to come and take me to Luther's. I am expecting a package. If I may, I will get any supplies you need, and get the mail."

"Lydia, make a list if you need anything." Will asked Martha and Kathy if they needed any thread.

After Earl had warmed himself by the fire with a cup of coffee, they set out for town.

Before supper, Paul asked Kathy if she would step into the parlor with him for a moment. Surprised Kathy followed him out. Paul gave her a smallbox and she opened it. There inside was a beautiful diamond ring. Paul slipped it on her finger and she said, "It's gorgeous, Paul."

"As you are, Kathy," said Paul and kissed her soundly. "Let's go show everyone."

"This makes it official," said Paul, proudly.

Will said, "We must drink a toast to Paul and Kathy! With coffee and milk." The whole group laughed and wished Paul and Kathy a bright future.

## Chapter

# SIXTEEN

March came in with roaring winds, whistling around the eaves with a howling noise. Will was worried. He got up about four a. m., and sat up the rest of the night. He made a fire fixed a quick breakfast. Then he saddled his horse at first light. He rode around his property to access any damage. All was well until he approached the shack that Kirby had built. It lay in shambles. The quilt lay in mud. A sheet was lying on a fence post across the pasture. "We have had one bad storm," thought Will.

He went back to the house. Both Kathy and Lydia were up. Will told them about the damage.

Kathy said, "This is awful, Will. I want to go home and see if everything's all right. Is it all right if Paul takes me to check on my family? I'm worried about them. I will come right back if they are all right."

Paul and Kirby came in and sat at the table followed by Martha and Dent. Paul said, "I'll take Kathy over to the Lawsons, Will."

After breakfast, Kirby went to milk and Dent to feed. Will was gathering limbs and debris from the front yard when he saw his buggy driven by Stella. He called out to Lydia to come. "Stella, what's wrong?"

"Will, can you send someone for the doctor? It's mama. She's hurt. Kathy stayed there with her."

Will rang the gong and Kirby came running. Will told him to saddle up and go for Dr. McDonald at once. "Lydia climb up, and I will go tell Martha to look after everything here. I will drive, Stella," he said. As they left the Wilson lane, going to the main road, he said, "Now tell us what happened?"

"The storm hit and made a terrible noise. Mother went out to the kitchen to see what was going on, and the wind caught her. She fell through the kitchen floor. The kitchen was collapsed. Part of the parlor wall is gone too."

"Where is Flora now?"

"Papa and I pulled her out and put her to bed. She hurts really badly, she says."

Will could see the damaged house before he reached the side road.

They found Flora on a bed covered with a quilt, with Sam and Kathy sitting with her.

"Are the children all right?"

Stella said, "I told them to stay in bed and we would bring them some food when we could."

Will asked, "What can we do to help?"

Sam asked Will, "Can you see if the fireplace chimney is safe enough to build a fire?"

"We will check it out. Have you been out to see about the barn?"

"No, I haven't left Flora." Just then the doctor drove in. He went directly in to Flora. He said to Sam, "Kirby has gone to get some help and will be along shortly."

Kathy said, "Paul has gone to see about the animals at the barn."

Dr. McDonald examined Flora. "Sam, Flora is badly hurt. She has a broken leg, and some internal injuries. She fainted when I pressed on her side. I think I will need a specialist. Can someone ride to New River to get Dr. Moore?"

"I can send Paul. Kathy, will you go find him, and tell him to come?"

Kirby drove up followed by a wagon filled with friends. Earl jumped down and whistled through his teeth. "What a mess!" he said.

Andrew Harness and Bitt Thompson were there and James Freeman, the banker's son. "They all left their work to come and help," said Kirby. Paul came in with Kathy. He told Sam the barn was damaged, but he had tied the animals to trees for the time being.

Will told him to unhitch one of the horses from his buggy, and ride to the farm for his horse, Thunder.

Dr. McDonald told Paul, "Dr. Moore has offices across from the General Store in New River. Do you think you can find it?"

"Yes," answered Paul.

"He lives above his offices, and if he isn't there, his nurse will know where he is."

Paul kissed Kathy good-bye and went out. Stella was crying again.

"Sam, I think the chimney is safe. Stella can build a fire and cook some boiled eggs over it and make some coffee."

Will went outside to tell the men what to do. "The debris must be moved so we can see how bad the floor is. It looks like where the stove is sitting is all right, but we will have to check the supports."

The doctor came outside. "Will I must go attend to my office. I have given Flora a sedative. I will be back before Paul can get back with the doctor. Then I can be free to stay with her."

Stella built a fire and found a pan and pot in the debris and washed them in spring water. She went to gather eggs and put some on to boil. Lydia sat with Flora and rocked the little girl, Dora. The other two Miranda and Hallie, went in and watched Stella cook the eggs and boil the coffee. Miranda said, "Will Mama be all right?"

"We think so. Another doctor is coming to help. You must be very good." Stella hugged her little sister.

Will examined the floor after the debris was piled under the trees. "It looks solid as I thought. Down here we need to extend the floor."

Kathy came outside. "Will, Lydia wants you to take her home and take the little girls so she can care for them. Stella is packing them some clothes."

Sam said, "Take one of my horses, Will, since yours is gone with Paul."

Lydia came out with the girls, and said, "Will, I will send back some hot food for everyone."

Kathy and Stella sat with Flora and prayed.

By the time Dr. Moore arrived with Paul. They had a fire going in the cook stove, for the chimney was still standing. Will put on water to boil in a pan he found. Earl and the other men picked out usable utensils and food that was packaged and set it all aside. "We came back on the train. We borrowed this buggy from the stationmaster. I left Thunder in Dr. Moore's corral."

Dr. Moore examined Flora. She lay pale against the sheets. Dr. McDonald had made a splint and set her broken leg.

Dr. Moore said, "She will have to be taken for surgery. She has some internal injuries."

Sam said, "Does that mean Knoxville?"

Dr. McDonald said, "Albany, Kentucky is closer. There is a wagon road to there that has been improved. We can use that."

"Put plenty of bedding in the wagon, and support her well." Sam carried her out, and it was decided that Kathy and Sam would go with them. They stopped by Will's to get two strong horses and put Sam's horses in the barn. Stella stayed with Lydia to help look after the children and help with cooking.

Will ate dinner and then took his wagon, loaded with a step ladder, a keg of nails, and a crow bar. Lydia and Stella packed baskets with hot food into the wagon bed.

"Put in some potatoes and onions to cook later," said Will. "We cleaned the stove up, and it is heating water now. Put in some lye soap, too. We have plenty towels as the bedrooms weren't damaged."

Lydia said, "I must lie down. I am very tired."

Will drove off and returned to the Lawson home. After the men had eaten, they went to the barn. Paul had already fed the stock. Will looked at the barn with a critical eye.

"The damage is not extensive but repairs are needed."

"What can we do?"

Will said, "We can't do any major repairs without talking to Sam. What can we do to make the cows and horses safe?"

Kirby said, "Put up temporary boards to keep the stock inside."

"We should prepare a place for the cows to be milked and a manger for feeding."

"We have a couple of daylight hours yet. Everyone round up all the boards and wood scattered by the storm. I will go drive the wagon up here with the ladder and tools."

Before dark, the stock were safely inside the barn and fed, and the two cows milked. Dent said, "I'll feed the pigs and chickens, and we can go home. We can leave the dog to guard the farm."

The next morning, Stella was frying bacon and eggs, while Martha set the table. Lydia was still lying down, feeling poorly. The strain had been hard on her, she said.

As the men were eating, the dogs announced Dr. McDonald. He stepped down from his buggy, and Will feared the worst.

"Come in, Doctor."

"Yes, I will."

"Have some coffee. Have you eaten?"

"No, I will have some coffee though. After it was poured by Stella's shaky hand, he looked up. "I have bad news. Flora started hemorrhaging and Dr. Moore could not save her." Stella stumbled to a chair, and Paul sat close. "We tried, Stella. She was just too badly hurt."

Paul led her off to the bedroom that she shared with Martha, and stayed with her. Will said "What is the plan, Doctor?"

Sam and Kathy are driving the wagon home. One of the hospital staff is driving another with Flora. Since the house is in such a state, we are sending her to the church. The funeral will be arranged and all will be over. Sam will have thought it all out by the time he gets to Norma."

Martha went to see about her mother. She called for Will. "Hurry, Papa, I think the baby is coming!"

Dr. McDonald rushed to Lydia, and rolled up his sleeves. Get some water ready and the baby's things. Immediately, he was in charge, and Lydia delivered a little girl. Martha carried it in to her father. Will sat with his new daughter and asked when he could go in to Lydia.

"The doctor will tell you. I am going to go tell Stella and Paul. Kirby was gone to do the farm chores. Dent was gone to check his traps in the woods. So when they both returned, Lydia was all ready to receive congratulations. Dr. McDonald said she must rest. "Remember, Will, her name is Caroline."


Sam and Kathy arrived and the funeral was arranged. People brought what decorations they could, mostly artificial flowers to the church. The family sat spent and dry-eyed for they had wept for so long it seemed they would never cry again. Pastor Green spoke to the people. A song was sung and Evie played the organ. Flora was buried outside in the church cemetery. Everyone went to Will's house, and the neighbors and friends brought dishes of food. Maggie came and sat with Lydia while Kathy and Stella cared for the little girls and tried to comfort Sam. He was bereft, and sat stonily by the fireside and barely ate any dinner.

In the afternoon, he told them he was going home. Kathy said, "We will all go, Papa. Come Dora---and we will get our things."

Three days later, Paul came to talk to Will. "Let's go outside." he said.

"I have been thinking, Will. Sam and Kathy need me. If we get married sooner, I can move in and help Sam with the property. He is so beaten down; I doubt he is even thinking what is best. Kathy and Stella are grieving too."

"Have you talked to Sam about this?"

"No, Sir. I think he will agree though. I can take some of the load off him. I know you can find another hand."

"That's no problem, Paul. I hate to lose you. You have been like a son to me."

"I appreciate your saying that. I plan to draw out some of my money I have been saving to buy land. I can use it to rebuild the house."

Will said, "Do what you think is best."

They went back inside. Paul asked to hold Caroline. "Who knows, Lydia, I may have one of my own sometime."

On Sunday, Paul went over to eat dinner with Kathy and her family. They were still struggling to cook on the stove that was exposed to the weather and trying to be careful that the children didn't fall off the edge where the boards had been torn away.

Paul said, "I will go with you to milk, Sam."

They got the milk pails and headed to the barn. When Sam was through feeding, Paul said. "I want to talk to you a few minutes in private, Sam."

Sam leaned against the fence and waited.

"You know I love Kathy very much and I respect you also. What would you think of Kathy and me speeding up our wedding date?"

"It is all right with me, Son. I have always wanted the best for Kathy, and you are the best as far as I am concerned."

"All right, when we are married, is it all right with you if we live here and you allow me to help you rebuild the kitchen? I promise to do a good job. I have told Will that I

113

want a year off to work on your property. I will draw out some cash from my bank to buy materials. It will be our home for a year at least, so I don't mind doing this."

"You are doing me a great favor. I will repay you in time what you spend on the house."

"Then we are agreed? Let's go tell Kathy."

Kathy agreed to the arrangement and was happy to have the wedding sooner than they had planned. She and Stella talked for hours about the preparations and what they would wear. It was announced in church. Kathy was given a shower and received many useful gifts, and some were for the new kitchen.

The little church was decorated with candles and ribbons and a few artificial roses and rosebuds. Kirby was the best man and Stella the maid of honor. Sam gave his daughter away, and Pastor Green did the honors.

They went directly to Will's house for a party and all the guests came too. Lydia was up and looking well, and Caroline was in the cradle that was a present to them. Kathy changed clothes and went to eat with Dora and her sisters. She was still their substitute mother. When Mr. and Mrs. Paul Redmond left the house they were showered with rice, and they left happily for their home.

There was so much to do to restore the Lawson house. Kathy, Sam and Paul sat down and drew plans. Kathy wanted a wide, long porch, and the girls wanted plenty of room. The entire kitchen had to be rebuilt and another porch there as well. Sam suggested a room over the kitchen for his bedroom. He wanted to be alone in another part of the house from the main family. He was still grieving for Flora. He was glad to have all the regular farm chores to do and that helped fill his days. At night he wanted to be in his private room. Paul and Kathy took over the main bedroom and the girls shared bedrooms. Malinda and Hallie shared one bedroom, and Dora shared her room with Stella when she was home.

It was decided that there would be a large kitchen with a pantry. Paul drew up the plans, and Sam approved. There would be back steps leading up to Sam's bedroom with its built-in closet. Hallie asked for a closet, too, and Dora wanted some extra shelves and a mirror.

Everyone helped. Long hours were spent, and Paul often had help from his friends. Sam would take long hours fishing and hunting when things got hectic No one minded, for they understood that he had to grieve in his own way. Paul and Kathy took the girls many times to put flowers on their mother's grave in the church cemetery and talk to them about her love for them.

Earl came and talked to Sam about some timber on his property. They went one Saturday through the forest and decided on trees to cut and which ones Earl would buy. For the added cash, Sam and Paul could build the rooms and porches, and fell trees of their own to season out in the sun.

Weeks later, they had their friends out from Norma to help with the barn. There were many much needed repairs there, and they needed the gaiety of an old-fashioned party to break the days of hard work.

Dora and Kathy spent hours canning vegetables from the fields and making apple butter. Malinda picked berries with her friends, and there were countless blackberry pies and jars of jelly made for the days ahead.

Lydia invited the entire family over on many Sundays while the new kitchen was being built and its overhead room. Kathy and Paul would tell the Wilsons of each new idea, and how things were shaping up.

Will said to Kirby, "I guess I am in the market for another farm hand."

Stella came back to work for Lydia. She was needed more than ever with Caroline to care for. Caroline charmed everyone she saw. Her shining eyes and smiling face made her a beautiful baby. Stella adored her.

The farm was busy with planting and sowing alfalfa, wheat and flax. Will cleared more of his forest land to grow corn.

Paul finished the new kitchen and added on two rooms complete with lofts and ladders leading up to them. He put a new roof on and built a large porch halfway around the house. His friend, Andrew, came over and helped some, and always took supper with them. His father and mother had come back to Norma to tend to the store, so he had time off every now and then.

Kirby built a rocker for Paul and Kathy as a wedding present, and Lydia made them a double wedding ring quilt. Dent told Paul that he was working on a present for them.

Sometime later he invited Paul and Kathy to come and visit. After they had eaten, Dent asked them to go with him to the barn.

"I have something to show you."

In the storeroom he led Paul and Kathy to a covered object. When he removed the cloth, a beautiful hand-made cabinet was revealed.

He said, "I drew the design from a cabinet at the Creech house."

"It's beautiful, Dent," Kathy said, and hugged him. Paul shook his hand.

"I think you have found your calling," he said. "It is a grand piece of furniture."

Will was sitting on the porch with Lydia and Caroline. "We have come a long way, Lydia. I can't imagine being any happier than I am right now."

"Enjoy it while you can. When this one grows up you are going to have to have all you can handle." At that moment Caroline reached up and gave Will a painful tug on his mustache.

# THE END